The door to Salem's room opened, and John stood there. . . .

For a long moment, they simply stared at each other. Then he took a step forward, the corners of his mouth curving upward slightly when she stepped back. "Losing your courage? You've come a long way to back off now."

"You surprised me, that's all. I didn't expect to see you until later."

His fingers curled around her arm. "I didn't expect to see you at all."

"Wyatt didn't tell you he called me, asked me to come home?" Salem asked softly.

"He said he'd called you. He didn't say you were coming back."

"You've got two crew members out because of the attack," she said, looking at his bruises and the cast on his arm. "I'm a qualified diver. I know you don't want me here, John, but you know you can trust me." She smiled faintly. "Even though I've been tempted often, I won't bash you over the head."

Something changed in his eyes as he slowly closed the distance between them. "You don't know what I want," he said roughly. She felt the hard fiberglass cast against the small of her back as his arms came around her. Tilting her head back, she parted her lips in surprise as he lowered his head.

Like a man who'd been thirsty for what seemed like forever, he drank from her mouth, drowning in her taste. The fires of passion had been banked too long for him to be gentle. Her body pressed against his as he kissed her long and hard. When he was with her, he couldn't think, only feel.

Pulling away, ⬚⬚⬚⬚⬚⬚ he buried his fac⬚⬚⬚⬚ have come back,⬚⬚⬚

WHAT ARE *LOVESWEPT* ROMANCES?

They are stories of true romance and touching emotion. We believe those two very important ingredients are constants in our highly sensual and very believable stories in the *LOVESWEPT* line. Our goal is to give you, the reader, stories of consistently high quality that may sometimes make you laugh, sometimes make you cry, but are always fresh and creative and contain many delightful surprises within their pages.

Most romance fans read an enormous number of books. Those they truly love, they keep. Others may be traded with friends and soon forgotten. We hope that each *LOVESWEPT* romance will be a treasure—a "keeper." We will always try to publish

LOVE STORIES YOU'LL NEVER FORGET
BY AUTHORS YOU'LL ALWAYS REMEMBER

The Editors

LOVESWEPT® • 432

Patt Bucheister
Tropical Heat

 BANTAM BOOKS
NEW YORK • TORONTO • LONDON • SYDNEY • AUCKLAND

TROPICAL HEAT

A Bantam Book / November 1990

ISBN 0-553-44063-2

Published simultaneously in the United States and Canada

Bantam Books are published by Bantam Books, a division
of Bantam Doubleday Dell Publishing Group, Inc. Its trade-
mark, consisting of the words "Bantam Books" and the
portrayal of a rooster, is Registered in U.S. Patent and
Trademark Office and in other countries. Marca Regis-
trada. Bantam Books, 666 Fifth Avenue, New York, New
York 10103.

PRINTED IN THE UNITED STATES OF AMERICA

OPM   0 9 8 7 6 5 4 3 2 1

Prologue

Salem was having a wonderful dream. She was floating free as a bird, soaring through the air, her fingers curled tightly around the thick ropes supporting the swing under her. Her hair was free of the tight braids Mrs. Stuyvesant made her wear, the long black tresses flying out behind her as she aimed her feet at the sky. Instead of the seaweed-green uniform she had to wear in the orphanage, her dress was a soft pink with ribbon bows down the front and a full skirt with two lace-trimmed petticoats beneath it. When the wind blew the skirt up, Salem laughed, not bothering to smooth it down.

In her dream, she wasn't eight years old. She was all grown up, which meant no one could tell her what to do ever again. Why she would be in a swing when she was no longer a child was a bit fuzzy, but that didn't take away the enjoyment. She was doing what she wanted to do, and that was a freedom she'd never had before.

Abruptly, like a balloon that had been pricked

with a pin, her dream exploded into nothing. Someone pressed his hand over her mouth and shook her shoulder, waking her.

She sucked in her breath, about to cry out, when a familiar voice whispered in her ear. "Don't make a sound, Salem."

She opened her eyes, still regretting being pulled from her dream, but not alarmed now that she knew it was John Canada who'd disturbed her sleep. In the dim light that leaked around the window shade, she could see his tall shadowy figure bending over her bed. At seventeen, he was almost twice her size.

"Get dressed as quiet as you can," he told her. "We're getting out of here."

She nodded, and he removed his hand from her mouth. Obeying orders was automatic for Salem. It was what she had done for as long as she could remember. The only difference between John's orders and the barked ones she usually received was she was more than willing to do as John asked. She trusted him as she trusted few people.

While she tugged her uniform dress on over her cotton nightgown, John pulled out from under her bed the long narrow box her clothing was kept in. He took the pillowcase off her pillow and stuffed in underclothing, a spare dress, and a sweater. When she realized what he was doing, Salem slid her hand under the mattress and withdrew a small tin box and a comb. She wasn't about to leave her treasures behind. It had taken her years to accumulate her worldly possessions of three dollars and sixty-two cents, a red ribbon, a rock with a delicate fossil of a leaf imprinted on it, a button she was positive was real silver, and a small bluebird made out of blown glass that

John and Wyatt Brodie had given her for her eighth birthday.

John accepted the tin box from her and added it to the pillowcase. He was one of the few she had shown the contents of the tin box to, and he knew each item was precious to her.

After she had fastened the last buckle on her shoe, she automatically placed her hand in his. He touched his lips with his forefinger to indicate the need to be very quiet. She nodded and followed him as he led her out of the dormitory. She glanced apprehensively at the several beds they passed, but the other girls remained asleep.

When they reached the stairs, they both carefully placed their feet to the right of each step, knowing the steps would creak otherwise. Salem tightened her fingers around John's hand when she stumbled on the last one. She was sleepy and disoriented, but she didn't once question going with him.

Her heart thudded loudly as they crept past Mrs. Stuyvesant's office, although it was completely dark. The director of the girl's dorm would be asleep in her room upstairs. Salem didn't know where John was taking her, but she knew Mrs. Stuyvesant would punish them both if they were caught out of their beds.

Wyatt was waiting for them behind the bushes near the front entrance of the cold brick building. As soon as he saw them slipping down the front steps, he picked up the two bundles at his feet and flung them over his shoulder. His usual cocky smile was absent, his young face reflecting his fear and excitement. At fifteen, Wyatt was old enough to understand the enormity of the giant step they were about to take, and young enough to be ignorant of the hazards that might lie ahead.

He took Salem's hand and kept pace with John's long strides as they headed for a break in the brick wall, hidden by a prickly holly bush. At night the high wrought-iron gate was locked, and they didn't stand a chance getting out that way. The thorny holly leaves tore at their skin and clothing as they shimmied through to the small break in the wall.

Wyatt went first, then helped Salem through the dark hole. There was another thick hedge on the other side, and he parted it for her small frame.

Before he followed them, John took a few seconds to look back at the large brick institution that had been his home for most of his life. He had never gone to bed hungry, nor had the staff ever been cruel. But every moment he had been there, he'd been aware of being a charity case. The state of Massachusetts had been his parents, providing for his care and his education.

The state of Massachusetts was also arranging for Salem to be adopted the following day, which was one of the reasons John was taking her away. Her impending adoption had forced him to put his plans into effect earlier than he had originally intended. In two months he would turn eighteen and would be released from the orphanage. He would have had to leave Wyatt and Salem behind, so he'd come up with the plan for all of them to leave.

A smile softened his hard mouth as he thought of his two young friends. The three of them formed an incongruous alliance in other people's eyes. Regardless of their age differences, though, they were the only family each of them had.

John raised his hand, touching his fingers to his forehead in a mock salute to the building. Feeling foolish for making the gesture, he turned to squirm through the hole.

Wyatt was holding Salem's hand tightly when John joined them. The little girl stood straight, her blue-gray eyes showing no fear or uncertainty as she clutched her meager bundle to her chest. John saw trust in those eyes as she looked up at him and felt something tighten in his throat.

Ever since he had picked her up on the playground after an older girl had pushed her down, he had been unable to resist the appeal of Salem's expressive eyes. From then on, she had followed him around. For someone who had always kept to himself, John found he liked the attention from the sassy little girl. She made him laugh, and he could be himself with her, without being defensive or on his guard. She didn't mind his quiet moods or his hot temper, content simply to be with him. She made few demands on him, other than companionship and loyalty.

It was that way with Wyatt too. The teenager had lost his parents several years before he came to the orphanage and had been farmed out to various relatives. When they couldn't control him or didn't want to try, he was turned over to the state. After a number of foster homes, Wyatt ended up at the orphanage. Small for his age, he was a prime target for the playground bully. The second time John had plucked Wyatt out from under a boy two years older than he, he took Wyatt to one side and started to teach him how to defend himself. Salem would watch them with her big dancing eyes but wouldn't interfere in the lessons. One day, she snatched several cookies from the kitchen under the cook's nose, and the three of them sat under a tree eating them. Salem proceeded to give a blow-by-blow account of the boxing lessons, mimicking John's instructions, and Wyatt's actions. The shared laughter wove a tight thread of companionship and warmth around them, uniting them in an odd fellowship.

From then on they were together during their free time, each needing something the other two provided. John couldn't envision life without Wyatt and Salem. He didn't even want to try. Whatever it took, he would do it rather than be without them.

He relieved Salem of her pillowcase, then took her hand. He and Wyatt automatically shortened their strides so she could keep up with them as they walked away from the orphanage, keeping to the shadows formed by the tall brick wall.

It had taken John six months of working at Bud's Gas Station to earn enough money to buy the second-hand car parked two blocks away. In his pocket was every cent he had left after making the last payment on the car. He only hoped the cash would get them to Key West, Florida, the destination he had picked out on the large map at school. It appealed to him as the farthest they could go without needing passports.

When they reached the dented old Chevy, he tossed their few belongings into the trunk. Salem crawled into the back where John had laid out a small pillow and a blanket. Wyatt joined John in the front seat, his eyes shining with the thought of the adventure ahead of them.

Hoping the fear clutching his stomach didn't

show, John glanced first at Salem in the rearview mirror, then at Wyatt. "If either of you have second thoughts, now is the time to tell me. Once I drive away from here, I'm never coming back."

"Good," Salem stated with feeling. "So start the car."

Salem's reflection disappeared, and he turned his head to look into the backseat. She snuggled her face into the pillow and pulled the blanket over her. Within seconds, she was asleep.

The sound of Wyatt unzipping his jacket brought John's attention to the younger boy. Wyatt jerked his head toward the road. "How fast does this buggy go?"

Grinning, John started the car. "Fast enough."

One

Sitting in the middle of her bed with her legs crossed under her, Salem Shepherd stared at the envelope in her hand, then at the bank draft that had fallen out of it. It was made out to her in John's distinctive handwriting, the amount triple what he'd sent her every month since she had started college in Seattle, Washington, four years ago.

She examined the inside of the envelope, carefully looking for a letter, a note, but there was nothing, just a narrow strip of paper with numbers after the dollar sign. The only thing remotely personal about the check was her name and John's signature, hardly an intimate means of correspondence.

After all this time, she thought, John should have eased the restrictions he had set between them. For four years, there hadn't been much communication from him, other than the checks. When she went back to Key West each summer, John rarely spent time with her, and never alone.

He had his work on the boats, and she worked in Delta's gallery, unless she was needed to fill in for a crew member. When she was in Seattle, she wrote John and Wyatt every week, occasionally more often when she was homesick. Once in a while, Wyatt sent her a postcard, rarely a complete letter. More often he would call to fill her in on the news on the home front and to find out how she was doing. Thankfully, his manner toward her hadn't changed. He was still part friend, part brother, and part lovable pain in the neck.

Occasionally John would add a brief note to his monthly check, acknowledging a letter from her or answering some question or other. Unlike Wyatt, he didn't phone just to chat. She hated the distance he felt had to be between them. It was all so unnecessary and useless—and painful.

Much had changed since that night the three of them had left the orphanage. They had been so young, ready to take on the world and managing to survive on stubborn determination. They had been like the Three Musketeers, one for all and all for one. Until she turned eighteen. Actually, the change had started earlier than that, when she was sixteen. John had started to withdraw from her physically, his affectionate hugs a thing of the past. She had been too young to know what had caused the shift in his attitude toward her. Later, when she felt the pull of physical desire herself, she began to understand. John was attracted to her but didn't want to be.

Because she hadn't been able to hide her feelings, she had been exiled to Seattle. At first, when John had suggested she go to college so far away, she had rebelled. Then she had welcomed the chance to prove she was capable of managing her life on her own, that she was an adult and not a child, as he kept insisting.

Salem stared down at the check, hating what it represented—that she was a financial obligation to John and nothing more.

Her landlady's granddaughter, who was helping Salem pack, was folding Salem's graduation robe when she heard the sound of paper tearing. Deanna Wong dropped the robe into a large box, then stepped over piles of books stacked on the floor to reach Salem's bed. Spotting the two scraps of paper lying on the bed, she picked them up and tried to piece them together. She sighed with relief. "A little tape and an understanding bank clerk, and you can still cash this."

Salem shook her head, the ends of her bluntly cut dark hair brushing her shoulders. "I'm not going to cash it."

"Why not? Your guardian has been more than generous. Why not take advantage of it? It will certainly make your life a lot easier the next couple of months."

Salem reached for the two pieces of paper and tore them again. It was the only outlet she had for her frustration, although it didn't make her feel any better.

"I don't want his money," she said, pain roughening her voice. "I want him to tell me to come home."

Deanna sank down onto the bed, ignoring the bits of paper fluttering to the floor. At eighteen, Deanna had the self-confidence and wisdom only the young think they have. "Maybe that's what he wants, too, but he thinks you would rather stay here. You told me you write glowing letters about the life you're leading here. He just might think you want to stay."

Salem's mouth twisted into a rueful smile. "John knows how I feel. I never made it a secret I didn't want to leave Key West in the first place. That hasn't changed since I've been here."

"I know," Deanna said dryly. "I've heard you complain every time it rains or the sun doesn't shine."

Suddenly restless, Salem sprang off the bed and walked over to the window. Rain streamed down the panes of glass. Wearing a pair of jeans and a heavy sweater over a shirt, she was still cold. She wrapped her arms across her rib cage for warmth as she watched rivulets of rain create crooked paths down the glass. There were many people in Seattle who liked the rain and cloudy days. She wasn't one of them.

Shivering with more than cold, she murmured, "I feel like I'm a prisoner whose sentence is just about up, but the warden won't allow me to go home."

"Have you committed some horrible crime you haven't told me about?" Deanna asked lightly.

"My crime was my age," Salem said softly, more to herself than her friend.

Deanna's dark almond-shaped eyes widened as she stared at Salem. "Excuse me?"

Salem shook her head, regretting mentioning it. It was the truth, though, the real reason John had sent her away. At least, one of them.

"I was supposed to broaden my horizons here in Seattle," she said, continuing to gaze out the apartment window. "The problem is, the only horizon I want to see is the one off the coast of Key West."

"Seattle isn't exactly purgatory, Salem," Deanna said, defending her hometown. "You have a few things to show for the four years in Seattle. You have a degree in marine biology, you've made a number of friends, received two marriage proposals, at least one indecent proposal that I know of, and not to put too modest a turn on it, you have a wonderful friend, namely yours truly. Unless you keep picking on Seattle. Then you can forget that part."

Salem turned from the window, unable to stand the sight of gray skies and rain when her heart and soul were yearning for sunshine and balmy breezes. "You have been a good friend, Deanna, and I'm going to miss you."

Pleased, the younger girl smiled. "I don't see why you have to leave right away. You know my grandmother will let you stay as long as you want. What are you going to do if you don't go back to Key West?"

"I don't know. I was going to go home for the summer, then take the job in Monterey if things didn't work out there. Now, I'm not sure what I'll do."

She sat down on the only chair that didn't have something piled on it. She and Deanna had been in the midst of packing when the envelope had arrived by messenger. When she recognized the handwriting, she had forgotten the stacks of clothes and books.

"The only thing that's kept me going the last four years," she said, "was the thought of returning to Key West and John and Wyatt. Now I'm getting the impression they are managing just fine without me, that my coming back would rock the boat."

"A unique turn of phrase, considering they own two boats."

"Three. Wyatt said they've recently bought a fishing trawler to use in some salvage work. They've subcontracted to find a shipwreck that is reputed to have millions of dollars in gold and silver in it. Being part of a crew that found treasure was how John got the money to buy his own boat when he was eighteen." She smiled. "I probably already told you about all that."

"A few times," Deanna muttered, not unkindly. She got off the bed and walked over to the dresser on the other side of the room. On top of it was a framed photograph of a much younger Salem standing between two men. They were all wearing shorts and T-shirts that had the name of their charter fishing business on the front, THE GYPSY FLEET. The tall dark-haired man on Salem's right was wearing sunglasses that effectively concealed his eyes. His expression was serious as he stared into the camera. The shorter man squinted into the sunlight, his blond hair in marked contrast to his deeply tanned skin. His smile was as carefree and confident as his stance.

"Since I've known you," Deanna said, picking up the picture, "you've talked freely about your home, living with that artist . . . What's her name?"

"Delta."

"Right, Delta. She runs a bed and breakfast, and you ended up living there permanently. You've told me all about fishing, diving, and boating in the Gulf, the type of food you miss that the Haitian cook fixes. I've heard about Delta's unusual penchant for staying up all night and sleeping during the day, and the way she dresses as though she's on her way to a safari in Africa. From your description of her, I could pick her out of a crowd, just as I could Wyatt from everything you've told me about him. But you never talk much about John Canada, other than meeting him at the orphanage and how he became your guardian when he was of legal age. I've gotten the feeling he's important to you in a way none of the others are, but you rarely even mention his name."

Salem stood and started packing books into a large empty box. "We had a disagreement before I left for college. We've never been able to get past it. It's painful to think about it, much less talk about it."

"It's a shame they all couldn't come to your graduation."

"John was there."

Deanna almost dropped the photo and grappled with it for a few seconds, finally setting it safely back on top of the dresser. Turning, she faced Salem, who was still calmly packing books. "You aren't kidding, are you?"

With a breath of a laugh, Salem said, "No, I'm not kidding. He was standing toward the back. He left after I accepted my diploma."

It took Deanna a few seconds to absorb what Salem had said. "Did you know he was coming?"

"John never said he would be here for my graduation, but I knew he would come."

"How did you know?" Deanna asked, still confused. "You just said you had this huge falling-out. Why would you assume he would come?"

"He wouldn't miss something this important in my life, especially when he wanted it for me more than I did."

"Where is he now?"

Salem shrugged. "I don't know. I checked the airlines, and there isn't another flight to Miami until early morning, so he's probably still in Seattle.

"Will you be meeting him later?"

Salem knew it was difficult for Deanna, with her large closely-knit family, to understand Salem's unusual background. "John obviously didn't want me to know he was here, so he won't be coming looking for me."

The box was full. She quickly taped it shut, then, having at last decided what to do, she walked over to her closet. From the back she withdrew a dress covered in loose plastic.

"I think I'll go conch hunting," she said quietly.

Deanna collapsed on the chair Salem had vacated. "I've known you for almost nine months, Salem Shepherd, and I only just now realized that you have lost your mind. I've had my suspicions in the past, like when you turned down Harry Burnside's offer to fly to Hawaii for spring break, but now I know for sure you have one wheel off your trolley. Why would you choose now of all times to go hunting for seashells?"

Salem removed the plastic and examined the dress critically. "A conch is a lifetime resident of Key West. For us, life began when we arrived in Key West, so we feel we qualify."

Deanna blinked several times as Salem's explanation sank in. "You're going to go looking for your guardian wearing that dress? You'll get arrested."

Salem grinned. "I don't think it will come to that. At least if I'm in this dress, John won't be able to think I'm still eight years old. Officially, he's no longer my guardian. I turned twenty-one a year ago."

"How do you know where to look for him? Seattle is a big city. He could be anywhere."

Salem draped the dress over the bed, then peeled her sweater off and began to unbutton her shirt. "It's simple. I'm going to call Wyatt. John would have told him where he's staying."

When she discovered that John had come to the graduation ceremony, Salem had expected him to call or drop by the apartment afterward. He had her address, even though he'd never been there. What she hadn't expected was an envelope delivered to the door instead.

He wasn't going to get away with thinking she could be bought off. He was going to have to face her. She wasn't going to let go of the most important person in her life without a fight.

A generously endowed waitress brought John another Scotch on the rocks, even though he hadn't finished the one he had ordered earlier. The man sitting across the table from him nodded at the waitress to dismiss her.

"I see you still have the same effect on women, John," Taylor Hanks said, chuckling. "She brought you a refill but not me, and I own this place."

John smiled faintly. "If I remember correctly, you were the one the girls followed home from the docks, not me."

"That's because you never asked them. We all figured you had your hands full with those two kids, and no time for women. Hell, you were a kid yourself. Of course, that didn't stop the babes from trying. I imagine that hasn't changed."

The Scotch was smooth and heated his blood as John took another sip. He hadn't been warm since he had gotten off the plane at Seatac Airport. Except when he'd seen Salem cross the stage to get her diploma. Then the blood had run hot and thick in his veins.

"I leave all that to Wyatt," he said.

Taylor laughed again. "So he does come out of the water now and then to see the ladies?"

"Occasionally."

"What about the girl?" Taylor asked, gesturing to the passing waitress for a refill. "When I came to Key West this winter, I didn't see her around. She had an unusual name as I recall."

Staring down into his glass, John felt a familiar tension tighten his muscles. "Salem."

"I remember her running down the dock every day to meet our boat when it came in. She was a skinny little thing with the sassiest mouth I've ever heard. What's she doing now?"

Driving me crazy, John thought grimly. "She just got her degree in marine biology." He couldn't help adding with pride, "She was in the top ten of her class."

"I'll be damned. It's hard to picture her sitting still long enough to open a book, much less read one."

John let his gaze roam around the waterfront bar with its nautical decorations. The decor wasn't original, but the place had a comfortable feel about it. Music was provided by a sound system, but later in the evening, Taylor told John, a small rock group would fill the even smaller stage at one end of the dance floor.

Bringing his attention back to Taylor, John said, "You told everyone you were going to invest your share of the treasure in a bar, but I never imagined it would be in Seattle, Washington. At the time I thought you were just kidding around like the rest of us."

Taylor shook his head, grinning. "How old were we, eighteen, nineteen? We had the world by the tail in those days, didn't we? It was pretty heady stuff to find all that gold and silver that had been in the bottom of the ocean for over two hundred years. Then when the skipper said he would give all the crew a share of the bounty, I couldn't believe my luck."

"Your luck seems to be holding up," John said. "The bar seems to be very successful."

"It's a living." Tilting his head to one side, Taylor said casually, "I was surprised when you called to say you were going to be in Seattle this weekend. Not that I'm not glad to see you. I just never thought you'd accept my invitation to come. I can't imagine anything important enough to pry you off Key West."

Even though Taylor hadn't come right out and asked him why he was in Seattle, the unspoken question hung in the air. The answer was simple. Salem. Coming to see her had begun as a temptation and grown into an obsession, one he could no longer fight. He had given in, using the excuse of seeing her graduate. Because of the demands of the charter business, it was impossible for both him and Wyatt to be away at the same time. As much as the younger man wanted to see Salem, John didn't give Wyatt the choice of coming with him. Wyatt would have expected to see her after the ceremony. That wasn't part of John's plan. Seeing her from a distance had been difficult enough. Being with her would make the ache worse.

Taylor didn't appear to expect an answer and his attention had shifted to something behind John anyway. For a moment he simply gaped, then he whistled softly under his breath.

Curious, John turned his head. His breath caught in his chest when he saw what, or rather who, had captivated Taylor. A dark-haired woman wearing a red silk dress was wending her way through the various tables. The dress was a simple sheath, leaving little to the imagination yet not blatantly provocative. Except perhaps in the eyes of the beholder. How had she known he was there?

In one hand she carried a small black purse and what looked like a thin book. Draped over her other arm was an embroidered black shawl, its long fringe swaying gently with each step she took. Her creamy shoulders were bare except for frail spaghetti straps that connected the front and the back of the dress. The soft shimmering material clung to her breasts, barely revealing their upper slope. Her dark hair skimmed her bare shoulders, the ends curving under slightly.

The only jewelry she wore was an antique Spanish gold coin about the size of a nickel hanging from a chain around her neck.

As she neared him, her gaze never left his face. Hot claws of need ripped through him when he saw the corners of her mouth lift in a smile. Damn her, he cursed silently. She knew exactly what effect that dress would have on him. And why not? he thought. He'd reacted the same way when she was enveloped from her neck to her ankles in the graduation robe.

His fingers tightened around his glass until it was in danger of being crushed as desire writhed and twisted inside him. But he didn't look away. He couldn't.

She stopped a foot away from him. "Hello, John."

He leaned back in his chair, giving the impression of being relaxed. "Hello, Salem."

She held out a leather-bound folder. "I thought you might want to see this, since you paid for it. If you'd stayed around after the ceremony, I would have shown it to you then."

He lifted his hand to accept the slim folder from her. Opening it, he saw it was her diploma. He shut it and handed it back to her. "You earned it. It's yours."

Ignoring it, Salem turned to the other man. He had stood up as she'd reached the table. She held out her hand. "We're being rude. I'm Salem Shepherd. You look familiar. Have we met?"

Taylor took her hand, acknowledging the introduction automatically while he continued to stare at her. "You're little Salem?"

Taking back her hand, she laughed. "I admit I'm not very tall, but at five feet five, I'm not exactly a midget either."

Taylor shook his head as though to clear it. "I meant little as in age, not height. I knew you when you were about ten years old. I'm Taylor Hanks. I was part of the crew that found the Spanish treasure just before the hurricane struck the Gulf Coast."

Aware of the interest Salem had aroused in the other male patrons in the bar, John stood and pulled out the chair between him and Taylor.

"You might as well sit down now that you're here."

"Why, thank you, John. Graciously put as usual."

She took the time to drape her shawl over the back of the chair and place her purse on the table. When John still held on to the back of the chair after she was seated, she looked up. There was a strained expression on his face as his gaze held hers briefly. She also saw awareness and arousal, and her heartbeat responded to both.

As John returned to his chair, the waitress came back with Taylor's drink and asked Salem if she would like anything. Salem asked for a white-wine spritzer, then glanced at John's nearly empty glass. "Bring the gentleman another Scotch."

"I've been ordering drinks for myself for quite a few years, Salem. I don't need you to do it for me."

She forced a smile. "It's good to see you too, John."

And it was. It seemed like forever since she had seen him last. His thick dark brown hair needed a trim as usual, touching the collar of the black slicker jacket he wore over a white shirt. She wondered how long it had taken him to remove the suit and tie he had worn to her graduation. Probably about thirty seconds. Tiny white lines radiated out from the corner of his eyes, laugh lines made more vivid by his tanned skin. Making the tough man laugh had been one of her main joys while she was growing up.

But he wasn't laughing now.

She shifted her attention to Taylor. "Now I remember you. You played the harmonica on the trips out to the dive site and back, rather badly I heard."

Taylor laughed. Sitting forward, he leaned his forearms on the table. "And I remember you were a nut-brown little girl who used to fly down the dock to meet the boat when it came in. You reminded me of a wild young gypsy." His expression changed, comprehension dawning. "The fishing fleet was named after you, wasn't it? The Gypsy Fleet."

"That was John's idea."

Taylor's gaze lowered to the gold coin visible above the low neckline of her dress. "I see you have a souvenir of the treasure we found."

Her fingers toyed with the coin as she met John's gaze. She remembered the coolness of the coin he wore when it had touched her heated skin the one time she had been in his arms.

She saw the expression in his eyes change from cool assessment to heated arousal. He was remembering the same thing.

"John had necklaces made for the three of us," she said.

A young sailor who looked about sixteen in his crisp new navy uniform and boot-camp haircut sauntered up to the table and asked Salem if she would like to dance.

She smiled up at him and rose from her chair. "I'd like that very much." As she hooked her hand through the sailor's arm, she said politely, "Excuse me," to the two men sitting at the table.

Taylor whistled softly as he shifted in his chair to watch Salem and her partner on the dance floor. "Good Lord, John. I can't believe she's that same little girl who used to cut bait and clean fish. She certainly grew up to be a beauty."

John couldn't help watching Salem, too, even though it hurt. It was like looking at a particularly bright sunset, wanting to see as much of it as he could before it disappeared. The sailor wasn't holding her tightly, but John wanted to tear the other man's hands away. The thought of any man touching her had kept him awake more nights than he could count. Actually seeing her in another man's arms was killing him by inches.

When the song ended, the sailor escorted Salem back to the table and thanked her for the dance. Another man approached with a hopeful smile, but John cut him off. His chair scraped across the floor as he shoved it back. Reaching down, he grabbed her arm and urged her to her feet. "Excuse us, Taylor."

He led her back onto the dance floor, walking to the center before stopping to pull her into his arms. The moment her breasts pressed against his chest, he knew he had made a major mistake. Looking at her was like dying. Touching her made him come alive.

His callused fingers curled around her smaller hand, as his other hand rested at her waist. She lifted her left hand to his shoulder. For a moment they didn't move, they simply looked at each other. Then he began to shift his feet to the slow rhythm of the ballad coming over the sound system, feeling her move effortlessly with him.

It was the first time he had danced with her. Wyatt had been the one to show her how to dance when she was a teenager. He shoved thoughts of Salem and Wyatt together out of his mind. These few minutes with her were his alone. They might have to last him a long time.

When another couple accidently bumped into

her back, pushing her against him, she didn't move away. She even followed him when he took a step back. The silky material of her dress slithered against his thighs, making him fully aware of the movement of her lower body.

Needing to put a barrier between them, if only in his mind, he murmured, "All those lessons with Wyatt have paid off. You dance very well."

She tilted her head back enough to see his face. "Wyatt tried only once to teach me to dance. The so-called lesson lasted exactly ten minutes. He nearly knocked my head off when he twirled me around, and he stepped on my foot three times. I told him to go dance with a barracuda. They have teeth to defend themselves with and no feet to stomp on."

"You were dancing with him last summer on the porch."

Salem searched his eyes, wondering why his words sounded like an accusation. She wasn't surprised when his expression gave nothing away. He was very good at hiding his feelings. "Our roles were reversed. I was trying to teach him to waltz. It's amazing to me how someone as graceful and coordinated as Wyatt is in the water can be such a klutz dancing." She chuckled. "Maybe he should leave his flippers on when he takes a woman out."

A corner of John's mouth slanted upward. "He would probably feel more comfortable than wearing a suit."

"Who taught you to dance?"

He slid his hand down to her hip to guide her away from a large man pushing a woman around the floor. Enjoying the feel of her sensuous movement beneath his palm, he had to drag his mind back to her question.

"I'm having my first lesson now."

Salem stopped dancing as she stared up at him. Amusement flickered in his eyes as he forced her to start again. Her bones were as soft as melted butter, and her heart rate skidded out of control with each brush of his hard frame against hers. And he'd never danced before. Now that she thought about it, she wondered why she'd been so surprised. Work filled most of John's days and nights, leaving little time for anything else.

"You learn quickly," she muttered.

The song ended, but John made no move to return to the table. There were things that had to be said in private. The middle of a dance floor would have to do.

His hands cupped her hips. "I didn't want you to know I was in Seattle, Salem."

She nodded. "I know."

Her calm statement surprised him. "I didn't plan on seeing you except at the graduation ceremony."

"I know."

"I came to your graduation because I wanted to see you accept the reward for four years of hard work."

"I know."

A soft instrumental melody began to drift around them. The other couples on the floor began to dance, but John wasn't aware of the music or the people.

"I'm proud of you, but you know that. You'll do well in that job you wrote about, the one at the marine museum in Monterey."

She could have throttled him. John Canada could take apart any engine and put it together blindfolded. He knew every fish, every tide, every current, and every coral reef in the area around the Keys. But he didn't know how much she'd hate going to Monterey rather than home. She met his gaze. Maybe he did know, she reconsidered. Perhaps he knew she had written about the job offer only to get him to tell her to forget California, to come home. Except he hadn't told her that at all.

"I'm not sure I'm going to take the job in Monterey," she said flatly.

"Did you get a better offer?"

Her fingers tightened on his shoulders. "Yes. Several, as a matter of fact."

He gave her time to continue, and when she didn't, he prodded. "Well? What are your offers?"

"Are you really interested or just making polite conversation?"

A muscle twitched in his jaw. "Do us both a favor, Salem,. Don't bait me. I'm not in the mood. Just tell me about the job offers you've had."

"One was from a university in Texas with a large biology department. The other was from a company in Key West, Porto Brothers."

John clenched his teeth at the mention of the charter fishing fleet that was his biggest competitor. "What in hell would the Porto brothers want with a marine biologist? They can't even spell *biologist*, much less know what one does."

"I didn't ask."

He didn't like the idea of the Porto brothers contacting her. Apparently, they had found out about her relationship with him and Wyatt.

"I don't remember the Porto brothers' fleet," she said. "Are they new to the island?"

"They arrived about six months ago. They have

two boats, and they're sharks, trying to take a bite out of everyone else's business."

She arched a brow in surprise at his harsh voice. "In the letter they sent, they made it sound like they had a big fleet."

"Did they contact you, or did you contact them?"

"They contacted me, and before you ask the next question, I don't know how they knew where I was or that I was getting a degree in marine biology. All I know is they offered me a job I turned down, although I admit it was tempting since it would mean I could work in the Keys." She met his gaze without flinching as she slid her arms around his neck. "I'm waiting for another offer."

He grabbed her wrists and brought her arms down. "We've been over this a hundred times, Salem. It's not a good idea for you to come home."

That was plain enough, she thought bitterly. Now she knew. It was why she'd come after him, to find out if she had interpreted the large check correctly. She had. It was a payoff. This time she wasn't going to stand toe-to-toe and argue with him as she had in the past. She always lost when she disagreed with John. Like now. His blunt words hadn't cut through her cleanly but painfully, roughly, rending her hopes like a jagged saw on tender flesh.

She jerked away from him and pushed her way through the other dancers, mindless of the people who stared after her. When she reached the table, she extended her right hand to Taylor. He'd been sipping from his glass and had to swallow hard as he clasped her hand.

"It was good to see you again, Taylor," she said.

"If you'll excuse me, I have to leave before I commit a felony on your premises."

Leaving the diploma on the table, she picked up her purse and shawl, and turned toward the door. Her throat was tight with suppressed anger and tears as she wound her way through the crowds of people standing in front of the bar. Finally she reached the door. Pushing it open, she pulled the shawl around her as the cool evening breeze off Puget Sound hit her heated skin.

She had taken three steps when a strong hand closed over her shoulder and whirled her around. John backed her against the outside wall of the building as he closed the distance between them, stopping only when his hard body was a breath away from hers.

"Damm it, Salem. Don't tell me you don't remember what happened the summer you were eighteen. I won't believe you."

"Of course I remember." Her voice was thick with anguish and unshed tears. She didn't want him to be aware of either. "We almost made love."

His fingers tightened cruelly. "No. I almost raped you."

Two

"It wouldn't have been rape, John," Salem said quietly. "I was more than willing to make love with you. If I remember correctly, I was seducing you, not the other way around."

He shook his head in denial. "You didn't know what you were doing. Luckily, I realized that in time and stopped."

"I didn't want you to stop."

He had to end this. "Dammit, Salem. I was your guardian. I was responsible for you, and I was tearing off your clothes like a madman."

It had taken her a long time to realize that to John, making love with her would have been dishonorable. Coming from a childhood in which he had little to call his own, his most valuable possession had been his pride and honor. Both had suffered four years ago.

But she had suffered too. The loneliness and frustrations of the past four years, of being shut out of the lives of the two people who meant everything to her, burst from her in an angry rush.

"That night you said I was too young to know what I was feeling, that I had misunderstood our relationship, that I didn't know what I was doing. You were wrong then and you're wrong now. I was eighteen, John, but that doesn't mean I was a child. I've never been a child. Neither Wyatt nor you nor I have ever known what it was like to be normal children. Circumstances made us grow up quickly, and made us aware of hardships in life that most people never experience. That doesn't mean I'm some sort of freak who doesn't know what love is."

Shock widened his eyes. "Salem—"

She pushed him away, surprised when he allowed it. "No. I won't let you tell me again that I don't know what I'm talking about. I've accepted that you don't feel the same way, but I'm still being punished because I stupidly confessed how I felt about you. I've spent four years getting a college degree like you asked, feeling it was the only way I could atone for the crime of wanting you. I've been punished enough, John. I want to come home."

John was stunned. He'd had no idea she had considered going away to college as punishment, that she thought her childhood had made her some sort of freak. Sending her away had been more than a punishment to him. It had been pure torture.

"If you'd stayed, we would have become lovers, Salem. You were too young, too sheltered to know whether that's what you wanted. You needed to experience more of life than you were exposed to on the Keys."

Shivering, she wrapped her arms around her waist. "I've been out with other men. I've been exposed to a variety of different people and situations. I have that experience you so badly wanted me to have." She felt a perverse satisfaction in seeing a glimmer of anger in his eyes when she mentioned other men. "I've even received two marriage proposals from men who obviously didn't consider me a child. I've done everything you told me to do. Except one. I haven't forgotten how it felt to be in your arms, how your tongue felt sliding against mine, the way my body fit yours when you held me."

He made a harsh sound, then stepped away from her. When he spoke, his voice was husky and rough. "Forgetting that was the most important thing you were supposed to do."

"I might as well forget to breathe as try to forget how I feel about you, John."

He shoved his hands into the pockets of his slacks, clenching them into fists to keep from touching her. Needing to put distance between them, he turned and took several steps away. "Nothing has changed, Salem," he said rigidly, gazing out at the dark water. "If you come back, you'll only be hurt. There can't be anything between us except friendship."

"Why?" she asked, her voice cracking with emotion.

"A number of reasons. One of them is you don't even know who you are."

The pain was so severe, Salem had to clasp her hand tightly over her mouth to stop her cry of anguish. She never expected John of all people to throw her lack of parents at her. Nor to use it against her. His circumstances had been the same as hers, yet hers weren't acceptable.

Pride stiffened her spine. She carefully adjusted

the shawl over her shoulders and took a deep shuddering breath before pushing herself from the wall. The first step away from John was the most difficult to take. The next was a little easier. She concentrated on watching her feet, willing them to keep moving toward her car parked around the corner. The smallest detail, a crack in the concrete, a tuft of grass growing near the curb, became important, something to analyze and dissect.

Anything to keep from thinking.

John didn't move for several minutes. He stared out at the lights reflecting on the dark water of the sound. He wanted to believe her. Even though Wyatt and his feelings still had to be considered, a large part of him longed to know that Salem still felt the same way, that she, too, desperately needed to share the heat of passion until they were engulfed in its flames. He closed his eyes for a moment. His own pain was easier to endure than causing pain to Wyatt, who cared for Salem too.

Steeling himself against the hurt he knew he would see in her eyes, he turned around.

"Salem, I—"

She wasn't there. He looked up and down the sidewalk, but there was no sign of her. She could have slipped back into the bar, but he doubted it. He struck the building with his fist in a useless display of anger. The only thing he accomplished was hurting his hand, but that pain was nothing compared to remembering the tortured expression in Salem's eyes.

Salem returned to the apartment to pack the last box into her compact car. Standing in the middle of the room that had been her home for the past school year, she looked around. Like the furnished dormitory rooms she had lived in for her first three years of school, the apartment had an anonymous look to it once all the personal items were removed. All that was left was serviceable furniture purchased for durability rather than style. The apartment had been a place to study, to sleep, and to keep her clothes. She had no sentimental attachment to it.

She bent down to pick up the last box. The phone rang. She was tempted to ignore it, as she had for the past three days. There wasn't anyone she wanted to talk to, especially Wyatt, and he was the only person who might be phoning her. She didn't want to talk to Wyatt yet. Not until she was settled in Monterey.

The phone rang for the third time. Glancing at her wristwatch, she decided Wyatt wouldn't be phoning her at ten in the morning, seven eastern time. At that hour, he would be on the boat.

She had barely said hello when Wyatt's voice blasted her. "Where in hell have you been? I've been trying to reach you for three days."

Her bruised emotions were still too tender to take any more abuse. "If all you're going to do is yell at me, I'm going to hang up, Wyatt."

"No," he practically shouted. "Don't hang up. I'm sorry. It's just that I've been worried about you, especially when I couldn't reach you."

"I've been busy. What do you want?" she asked bluntly.

For a moment, there was only silence on the line. Then Wyatt asked, "What in hell happened when John came to your graduation?"

"Why not ask him?"

"Because I would just as soon keep my head attached for a little while longer. He's been like a keg of dynamite ever since he got back. It doesn't take much to make him explode these past three days, especially after the boat was sabotaged and he and two of the crew were beaten up."

Salem's fingers tightened on the phone. Her heart thudded so painfully, she couldn't speak.

When she didn't say anything, Wyatt explained. "It happened the night John got back from Seattle. Evidently, the Porto brothers thought he was still out of town when they decided to put a crimp in our operation. They poured sugar in the gas line of *Gyspy I* after beating up Carlos, Arlo, and John, who were all on the boat when the Porto brothers' men showed up. Carlos and Arlo are still in the hospital, and that's where John should be, but he wouldn't stay there."

She had to know. "How badly was John hurt?"

"A couple of bruised ribs, a bump on the head, and a broken wrist. Enough to keep him from diving. You can imagine how well he's taking that."

"Why would the Porto brothers try to sabotage the boats and beat up the crew?"

"It's too involved to go into now. We'll fill you in when you come home. We really need you. We've bled the lines and are overhauling the engine, but it's put us behind schedule, and we're short-handed. How much longer are you going to take to finish up there and come home?"

"I wasn't planning on coming back." She was amazed at how much it hurt to say it aloud. "I'm going to work in California. I've been offered a job that starts in September. I'm leaving today to drive down there and find a place to live. Then I'll get a job to tide me over for the summer."

The line sizzled with a few soft-spoken expletives. "You have a job here. Dammit, Salem, you belong here, not in California." After a brief pause, Wyatt added, "I know there's some problem between you and John. I'm not totally blind. I've seen the way you both skirt around each other when you're home. Can't you put it aside for now? We need to stick together, or we're liable to lose the charter business. You said you didn't have to start your job until September. At least come home for the summer. We need to hire a couple more divers, but we're not sure who we can trust at this point. You're a qualified diver. You could go in John's place. Besides, I can't handle John's temper as well as you can. Next time he might not be so lucky. Next time he could be seriously hurt, especially if he goes looking for trouble with the Portos, and that's the kind of mood he's in."

She was torn between the desire to go home and concern over the complications it would cause between her and John. He had made it clear how he felt about her coming back. "Does John know you're calling me?"

It was obvious by Wyatt's hesitant reply that he was reluctant to give her an answer. He had never lied to her in the past and didn't now. "I told him I've been trying to reach you," he said evasively. What he didn't tell her was that John had been asleep at the time.

Not entirely satisfied with Wyatt's answer, she put her question another way. "Does John know you're asking me to come back?"

"I told him that too."

"And?" she asked impatiently.

"He didn't tell me not to."

A beggar at the door can't be choosy with the handout he receives, she thought. Whether John was rolling out the red carpet or not, she wanted to go home. If what Wyatt said was true and John was in danger, she would never forgive herself if she stayed away out of pride and something happened to him.

"Has Delta rented out my room?"

Wyatt sighed with profound relief. "Your room is always there for you. You know that. How soon can you get here?"

She figured the distance and the fact that she would be driving alone. "It will probably take me five days if I push it."

"What the hell are you going to do? Come by covered wagon? We could all be at the bottom of the ocean in five days. I know John left you some money. Why can't you fly?"

"I tore up the check."

He whistled softly. "That must have been some blowout the two of you had. It doesn't matter about the check. I'll phone the airline and have a ticket waiting for you at the airport. Bring a suitcase of clothes you need and ship the rest of the stuff. You won't need your car when you get here. You usually walk anyway, and there's always a Jeep you could use if you've gotten lazy in the big city."

Salem found herself smiling. Some of John's dictatorial ways were rubbing off on Wyatt. Excitement battled with apprehension as she seriously thought about going home. It might mean rejection, having to accept being near John but never close to him. The past three summers had shown her it was painful to see him daily, if even from a distance, but being away from him hadn't been any easier. They certainly didn't stand a chance of working out their problems if she was in California and he was in Key West.

It wasn't like her to give up. Life had taught her that she had to work for what she wanted rather than sitting back and wishing for it to appear. The pain of John's rejection had made her forget that. It was time to put away the hurt and humiliation, and fight for her right to love him.

"I have enough money for an airline ticket, Wyatt."

"It's about time one of you came to your senses," he muttered. "Let me know what flight you'll be on and I'll meet you."

"It sounds like you have enough to do." Now that she had decided, her plans fell into place. "I'll find my own way to Delta's. Tell Connie and Delta to expect me either tomorrow or the next day at the latest. There are a few things I have to take care of here."

"Okay, brat. I'll see you soon."

Salem grinned as she hung up the phone. Wyatt had always called her brat and probably always would, no matter what her age. It used to make her angry when she was younger, especially when the term had fit her behavior and she had known it. It hadn't been easy to hold her own against John's autocratic manner and Wyatt's continuous teasing, and occasionally she had been very bratty.

She glanced at her watch, feeling valuable time slipping away. Now that she had decided to return to Key West, she was anxious to be on her way. It was too early for Deanna to be visiting her grandmother, but Salem needed to get in touch with her to see if the younger girl was still interested in buying her car. Maybe Mrs. Wong would know where Deanna was.

She rushed out of the room, yelling, "Mrs. Wong!"

Salem landed in Key West in the late afternoon of the following day. She carried her luggage out of the terminal building, even though she was practically staggering with fatigue.

It has been late the previous night before Deanna could come over to discuss buying Salem's car. They had agreed on a price, and Deanna had even offered to take care of shipping Salem's belongings for her. Then the car had to be unpacked and her suitcases repacked. When she finally did go to bed, she'd been too excited to sleep. Even though she tried to push the doubts away, they kept edging forward in her mind as she spent the last night in her apartment. As much as she wanted to go back, she wasn't sure how much she could take if John ignored her as he had in the past.

After hailing a taxi and giving the driver Delta's address, she sat back to look out the window at the palm-lined streets and the gingerbread mansions characteristic of the island. Only three and a half miles long and one and a half miles wide, Key West was the last island in a chain of small narrow pieces of land extending 150 miles southeast of the tip of Florida. The Spaniards had called it the Island of Bones. To her, it was home, the only one she'd ever had, the only one she had ever wanted.

The driver stopped in front of the large white clapboard house nestled among palm trees and a thick profusion of shrubs and flowers. A white picket fence extended around the property, stopping at a paved driveway. Eight wooden rocking chairs painted a pleasant emerald green sat on the open covered porch that extended across the front of the house and along one side. The windows glistened in the bright sunlight as Salem hauled her suitcases up the drive to the side door.

Although it was late afternoon, Delta would undoubtedly still be in her bedroom, so Salem didn't expect to see her until later. And since there were still several hours of daylight left, she didn't expect either Wyatt or John to be waiting to greet her. Leaving her luggage in the small utility room, she entered the kitchen. The scene was so familiar and so welcome, she felt her throat tighten with emotion.

Connie Dubacca, the Haitian cook and housekeeper employed by Delta for so long as Salem could remember, was kneading bread dough with her thick brown hands. The assortment of bracelets Connie always wore jangled as she hummed softly. Both sounds were as familiar to Salem as the white scarf wrapped several times around the older woman's proud head and her white shirt worn loosely over a full beige skirt that fell to her ankles. Sensing her presence, Connie looked up and smiled at Salem.

As though Salem had only been gone a couple of hours, she said simply, "Hello, child."

Salem walked over to the worktable and kissed

Connie's cheek. "Hello, Connie. How have you been?"

"As good as can be expected. If Mr. Wyatt hasn't eaten them all, there are some ginger cookies in the jar. I don't suggest you eat too many though. You'll ruin your dinner."

Smiling at the gentle warning, Salem shook her head. "I'll wait." Wondering if the arrangements of the past were still in effect, she asked, "Are Wyatt and John expected for dinner tonight?"

"Now where else would they eat? Of course they'll be here."

Salem decided to take advantage of the time before dinner to put away her things and prepare herself for meeting John again. She couldn't expect his welcome to be as casual or as automatic as Connie's.

"Is Delta still in her room?"

"I took up a pot of tea about ten minutes ago, so she'll be stirring herself soon."

Salem fetched her suitcases. "I'll be up in my room unless you want me to help with the dinner."

The bracelets clattered as Connie waved a floury hand toward the door. "You run along, child. I have dinner well in hand, but if you wish to set the table later, it will be most welcome. We have six guests this week."

Nodding, Salem left the kitchen, passing through the dining room to reach the hall. One of the suitcases bumped against the railing as she tugged them up the stairs. When she reached the top, she walked across the polished wood floor to another set of stairs that would take her to the third floor. The four bedrooms on the second floor had originally been set aside for tourists to provide an income for Delta after her husband passed away twenty years earlier. Her paintings had been selling well for the last ten years, but she still took in guests, though more for the company than to supplement her income. The older woman enjoyed chatting with the guests in the evening before they went off to bed and she went to her studio behind the house.

Delta'a private quarters were on the third floor, along with the room she reserved for Salem and a spare room where personal friends stayed. John and Wyatt had moved into a small cottage nearer the docks shortly after John had bought the first boat. Salem had stayed at Delta's.

The door to her room was ajar, and Salem nudged it open with her elbow. She dropped the cases on the floor at the foot of the brass bed. Running her hand over the cool metal, she glanced around the room. New fabric covered the window seat where she had spent many hours reading, dreaming, and gazing out at the ocean in the distance. The clamshell quilt covering the single bed had been made by Delta's mother many years ago. The oak dresser along one wall and the chest of drawers against another gleamed in the bright light coming through the window.

Some of her tension eased as she absorbed the homey atmosphere of the room she had used since she was a child. Needing to feel she was actually going to stay, she hefted first one suitcase, then the other onto the bed and began to unpack. Once that was accomplished, she left the room to go to the bathroom next door. Her hand was on the latch when she heard the sound of running water through the closed door. She knew it couldn't be Delta. She had her own bathroom in her quarters. When Delta had friends staying in the spare room, Salem shared the bath with them. Connie had said there were six guests, but Salem had thought she meant tourists who would be using the second-floor facilities. Obviously, not all the guests were tourists.

She removed her hand from the latch and was turning away when the door opened. She didn't know who was more surprised, she or the man who stood in the doorway. The last person she'd expected to see was John, and he apparently felt the same way.

Dressed in faded jeans and a cotton shirt open down the front, he stood stiffly, his expression guarded. An angry-looking bruise marked his temple near the hairline. A white fiberglass cast ran from beneath his elbow over his right wrist and his hand, leaving his fingers and thumb uncovered.

For a long moment, they simple stared at each other. Then John took a step forward, a corner of his mouth curving slightly when she stepped back.

"Losing your courage?" he murmured. "You've come a long way to back off now."

"You surprised me, that's all. I wasn't expecting to see you until later."

His fingers curled around her arm, and he drew her into her room. "I wasn't expecting to see you at all," he said. "I've been staying in the spare room for the last three nights."

He shut the door behind them and led her to the window seat. As she sat down, she watched as he moved several feet away. He hadn't been expecting her, which meant Wyatt had lied to her. She found that difficult to accept. Almost as difficult as knowing John wasn't pleased to see her, even though she'd anticipated that.

"Wyatt didn't tell you he called me, did he," she asked.

"He said he had called you. He didn't say you were coming back."

It was important for him to know she'd been invited, even if it wasn't by him. "When I asked him if you knew he was asking me to come home, he said he told you."

"If he did, I was unconscious at the time."

Her gaze went to the bruise on his forehead, then to the cast. "He told me about the attack."

"He shouldn't have."

"Well, he did," she said with a hint of temper. "He understood that I had a right to know, which obviously you don't. He also thought I could be of some help, so he asked me to come home."

John planted his hands on his hips, his legs spread apart in an aggressive stance, the cast starkly white against his tanned upper arm and chest. "How in the hell did he figure that?"

"You have two members of your crew out of commission at the moment, due to their injuries." She glanced at his cast again. "You can't dive with your wrist in a cast. You could hire other divers, but how would you know they weren't on the Portos' payroll? I'm a qualified diver. You taught me yourself, so you know I can do what has to be done. I realize you don't want me here, John, but you know you can trust me." She smiled faintly. "Even though I've been tempted several times during the last couple of years, I won't bash you over the head."

Something changed in his eyes as he slowly closed the distance between them. He reached for her with his good hand, drawing her to her feet. "You don't know what I want," he said roughly.

She felt the hard fiberglass cast against the small of her back as he slipped his arms around her. Tilting her head back, she started to speak, but then he covered her lips with his.

Like a man who had been thirsty for what seemed like forever, John drank from her mouth, drowning in her taste. The fires of passion had been banked too long for him to be gentle. Oddly enough, gentleness didn't appear to be what she wanted, and she went up on her toes to meet his desire with urgent needs of her own.

Her soft body molded to his. The cradle of her femininity pressed against his aroused body as he kissed her long and hard. His mind clouded with wanting her, desire obliterating everything else that had seemed so important. When he was with her, he couldn't think, only feel.

Drawing badly needed breath into his lungs, he buried his face in her neck. "You shouldn't have come back, Salem."

Putting more faith in his actions than his words, she murmured, "We have to settle this thing between us, John. One way or the other."

With an effort, he raised his head and loosened his hold on her. "I thought we had settled this in Seattle."

"It was settled in your mind, not mine."

He looked at her but didn't speak.

She missed having his arms around her, but wasn't suffused with the desolation she had felt before when he'd withdrawn from her physically. Now she knew he still wanted her, even if he was fighting it and her.

"When I was growing up," she said, "one of the

things you stressed was that life always presents us with choices, and it's important to make the right choice when the time comes. I've made the only choice I could make, John. I came back. This is my home. This is where I belong. If you can't accept that, I'm sorry."

He drew the back of his forefinger along the soft skin of her cheek. "God help me, but I can't send you away again. I should. It would be the wisest thing I could do for everyone, but I can't."

The sound of footsteps in the hall reminded them that they weren't alone in the house. John dropped his hand.

For the first time in what seemed like forever, he gave her a smile of warmth and affection. "You always were a stubborn little girl. That hasn't changed."

He walked to the door and opened it, but hesitated when she spoke his name. Keeping his hand on the latch, he turned to look at her.

She kept her voice even, her gaze serious. "I might not come with a pedigree, but I do know who I am, John."

His eyes drilled into her, their expression puzzled. He dropped his hand from the latch and started back toward her. Delta called to him from the doorway. He shook his head in frustration and left the room.

Misunderstanding the negative movement of his head, Salem swallowed defeat. Again.

Three

Salem didn't see Delta until she had showered and changed into a pair of white shorts and a blue knit top. The older woman was dressed as usual in a large shirt and skirt, similar to the loose clothing Connie preferred except that Delta liked safari-style shirts and didn't wear jewelry of any kind.

Even though she was as warm and welcoming as ever, Salem was concerned when she noticed Delta moving more slowly, her steps smaller and almost cautious. There was more gray in Delta's fading blond hair than Salem had remembered, and occasionally she saw a strained expression in Delta's blue eyes, as though she were experiencing some discomfort. For the first time Salem became aware of Delta's advancing age. Calculating quickly in her head, she realized Delta had to be in her late sixties or early seventies. Her spirit was as young as ever. It was her body that was growing older.

Dinner that evening was a festive occasion as

Delta welcomed Salem back into the fold. The artist didn't adhere to the practice of gobbling down food but preferred to have leisurely meals, with conversation as important as the food. Instead of the usual wine, she had unearthed several bottles of champagne and poured liberally, ignoring frowning glances from Connie, who disapproved of alcoholic beverages.

While they ate, Delta regaled the guests with various stories of Salem's growing up on the island. Some of the incidents were embellished beyond belief, but the guests were entertained, which was Delta's intention. While Wyatt, John, and Salem were accustomed to the older woman's penchant for exaggeration, it was obvious by the occasional startled glance in Salem's direction that the tourists believed every word she said.

Several times Salem saw John's expression soften and amusement flicker in his eyes. She also noticed how he kept his injured arm across his middle, his hand holding his side. His bruised ribs were obviously bothering him. His appetite seemed to have deserted him, too, as he only picked at the food on his plate.

Sometime between the conch chowder and the steamed shrimp, Wyatt began contributing to the stories. Salem turned the tables on him by telling the guests about a large barracuda that seemed to find Wyatt whenever he was diving. They could tell it was the same fish by the scar on its right side made by a fishhook. Nicknamed Dufus, the fish would swim directly in front of Wyatt's mask and stay there, staring and poking at the glass. Each time Wyatt attempted to push the large fish away, Dufus would simply evade his hand and return to his position in front of the mask. Swimming away didn't help either. Dufus just swam along with Wyatt.

One of the guests, an amateur diver who was taking scuba lessons, asked Wyatt, "Why didn't you feed it? Maybe that's all it wanted."

"A barracuda can snap a lobster in half in one bite," Wyatt answered. "Feeding a predator fish is not a good idea if you want to keep your fingers."

"So what did you do?"

Salem glanced at John, who was sitting across the table from her, and smiled, pleased when a corner of his mouth lifted slightly in response. Turning to the man who had asked the question, she answered for Wyatt. "He took a net bag down with him, small enough so Dufus couldn't have room to bite through the plastic netting and large enough so he could still move around. Wyatt would catch Dufus in the bag, then weight it down with a rock after tossing a couple of fish inside. Just before Wyatt went to the surface, he'd release Dufus. After being imprisoned in the bag several times, Dufus finally took the hint and left Wyatt alone."

Wyatt accepted the laughter with his usual good nature. "It's the first time I ever saw a fish give me a dirty look."

"Do you dive also, Miss Shepherd?" the man's wife asked Salem.

"Yes. In fact I'm going to crew on the *Gypsy II*, starting tomorrow." She could feel John's displeasure as he stared at her, but she went on. "When the boat can't go out due to the weather, I'll work in Delta's gallery."

"Only for the summer," John added, his gaze holding hers. "Then she goes to Monterey, California, to work at a marine museum there."

"The one near Cannery Row?" the woman exclaimed. "We've been there. It's a fascinating place."

Her husband agreed, which led to a discussion of other attractions the couple had seen.

After the dessert of key lime pie, Delta encouraged the guests to have their coffee outside on the porch to watch the spectacular sunset. Reminded of mice trailing after the Pied Piper, Salem watched the guests follow Delta from the dining room. Wyatt and John remained at the table as usual to finish their coffee. In the past, Connie usually joined them once the guests had left, and they would quietly discuss the events of the day and any problems that might have come up. It had been Salem's favorite time of each day, when they were all together for an hour or so.

But tonight Connie served their coffee and returned to the kitchen, making Salem wonder if the cook knew something she should know. She pushed her chair back and began to stack the dishes until John ordered her to stop.

"Leave those for a minute and sit down."

She sat back down, crossing her arms in front of her. It wasn't worth debating whether she wanted to sit down or clear the table. She knew he hadn't been happy when she made her little announcement earlier. Now she was going to find out just how unhappy he was.

Instead of directing his attack at her, though, John turned to Wyatt. "What about those two men Arlo recommended?"

"Neither one is available."

"How close is Tony to getting certified?"

Wyatt grimaced. "Not close enough. He isn't really serious about following the rules, much less willing to take a test." Before John could ask about any other divers, Wyatt said, "We need a diver tomorrow. I've been on my own for the last three days, and I haven't covered half the area we had scheduled to go over each day. Our contract with the salvage company states only certified divers can be employed. With Arlo, Carlos, and you unable to dive, that leaves just me. We need Salem, John. Not only is she certified, but she knows how we work. Plus we can trust her. The rest of the staff can take care of the charters lined up with the other boats, but none of them fit the requirements the salvage job needs, and you know it."

John knew it, but he didn't like it. He turned to gaze at Salem. Risking his own safety and Wyatt's was one thing. Putting Salem in danger was something else. There were plenty of divers who could do the job, but he was reluctant to hire anyone he hadn't worked with before or trusted. He also didn't want to renege on the contract and have it taken over by the Porto brothers. His pride fought with his protective instincts. In order to satisfy both, he would just have to make sure extra precautions were made to keep Salem safe.

He picked up his cup of coffee. "Since the *Gypsy I* isn't ready to go back out yet, get Bubba to go out with you and Salem tomorrow."

Wyatt ran his fingers through his blond hair, obviously not pleased with John's suggestion. "We don't need anyone riding shotgun. We already have Charlie handling the boat, and Pierre is the deckhand. If anyone tries to board while we're in the water, they could handle it."

"Bubba goes."

Having heard that particular tone of voice

enough times, Wyatt knew he had to give in. "All right. Bubba goes." Grinning at Salem, he added, "With Bubba along, we don't need to worry about ballast. Or our lunches. That guy can put away more food than a hungry shark. If the Porto brothers try to come aboard, we'll have Bubba sit on them."

John wasn't through with his instructions. "If you have any problems, call me on the radio. I'll be at the cottage."

Nodding, Wyatt picked up his coffee, then winked at Salem. She knew he was taking the threat of trouble seriously, but was more than willing to meet it head-on. She was also aware that John wouldn't be sending an extra crew member along if she wasn't involved. At least she was going to be allowed to go, even if John wasn't terribly enthusiastic about it.

Without making any comment, she again rose from her chair and picked up the stack of dishes. She started walking toward the kitchen but stopped when John called her name.

Turning her head, she met his gaze directly. "Yes?"

"At the first sign of trouble, I want you to get the hell out of the way. Do you understand?"

"Completely."

For a long moment, he stared at her, his expression unreadable. "It's been a while since you've dived. Take it easy tomorrow."

She nodded and was about to continue to the kitchen when he added, "I'll be returning to the cottage tonight."

She smiled briefly. "I figured you would."

This time she didn't wait to see if he had anything more to say. She didn't need it spelled out why he was going back to the cottage. He was willing to face Delta's displeasure by leaving before his injuries were healed because she was there now. He didn't even want to be under the same roof with her. Telling herself not to be hurt didn't do much good.

She returned to the table several more times, ignoring the two men as she removed dishes. Each time she entered the dining room, she was aware of John's intent gaze on her, but she didn't look at him. She felt as though she were walking a very thin tightrope. One misstep and she could lose her balance.

Once the table was cleared, she remained in the kitchen to help Connie with the dishes. She wouldn't subject herself any longer to the torture of being in the same room with John when she knew her presence irritated the hell out of him.

She was sitting at the small table in a window alcove having a second cup of coffee with Connie when Wyatt entered the kitchen. He walked over to the ceramic cookie jar on the counter and removed a handful of ginger cookies.

Ignoring Connie's frown, he said, "I'll be by around six to pick you up tomorrow morning."

She nodded. "I'll be ready."

"We're heading back to the cottage now. I don't suppose you would like to try to convince John to stay here one more night?"

"No, I wouldn't." She glanced at Connie, whose frown had deepened, then looked back at Wyatt. "Why? Does he need special care because of his injuries."

Wyatt shrugged. "I don't know. He's been staying here since he was hurt. Delta and Connie have been taking care of him."

Salem shifted her attention to the cook. "Connie?"

"We thought it best he stay here after the attack. Because of his head injury, he was to be awakened every two hours the first night. Miss Delta and I took turns waking him, making sure he took the medicine the doctor gave him in the hospital. Apparently, he still does not sleep well. Miss Delta said she sees the light in his bedroom when she looks out the studio window during the night. I have heard him pacing when I have gone past his room."

Salem started to push back her chair, ready to confront John. His health was more important than the rift between them. If he still needed care, he should stay at Delta's. She would tell him she'd go the cottage instead of him if he wouldn't stay because she was under Delta's roof too.

Connie reached across the table and put her hand over Salem's, stopping her. "No, child. Let him be. Sometimes the sickness that keeps a man from sleep is not from a blow to the head, but one to the heart. Let him be. He will have to find the cure in his own way, in his own time."

Wyatt shook his head in bemusement. "I'm not even going to try to decipher that kind of logic." He walked over to the table and ran his forefinger down Salem's nose, then kissed her cheek. "It's good to have you home again, brat."

The affection in his voice made Salem feel oddly tearful. She stood and slipped her arms around his neck, burying her face in his chest. "Take care of him, Wyatt," she said softly.

"Don't worry. He'll be fine. He's tough."

Neither one was aware of John standing in the

doorway watching them. Nor did they see him turn away, his eyes bleak and empty.

For the next two days, everything went smoothly. Salem reveled in the joy of being back in Key West, especially out on the crystal-clear water with the sun on her skin. Her wetsuit fit perfectly, the weightbelt heavy at her waist until she went into the water. It was sensible to wear a wetsuit since the body temperature lowers after some time in the water, even in tropical water. Wyatt preferred to wear only the top of his wetsuit with a pair of swimming trunks, gloves, and flippers. Salem's preference was a top with short sleeves and a bottom that extended to her knees. Underneath she wore a bikini, so she could strip off the wetsuit after a dive.

She felt no awkwardness during her first dive, even though it had been a long time since she'd been in the water. She followed Wyatt's instructions, covering the allotted area under the sea as she looked for signs of a shipwreck—ballast stones, cannonballs, olive jars, iron barrel hoops. Ballast stones were the easiest to spot, some being thirty inches in diameter and weighing up to a hundred pounds. It was time-consuming and tedious work, for the strong current, hurricanes, and other storms made it enormously difficult to find wrecks on the ocean floor. The occasional sighting of gold coins or a matchlock musket piece encouraged crews to keep searching.

Many ships had been wrecked off the Keys over the last three hundred years. In 1733, records showed, seventeen ships had gone down during a hurricane, with an estimated treasure of sixty million dollars. It was one of those ships the Gypsy Fleet had contracted to find.

The only dark cloud on her horizon was that she had no contact with John, other than occasionally hearing his voice on the radio. Each night she expected him to come to Delta's for dinner, but he didn't. When she asked Wyatt if John was all right, the only response she got was a shrug.

On the third day, everything went wrong that could go wrong, except for the weather. Salem and Wyatt came up empty-handed dive after dive, and by the end of the day were more than ready to go back to shore. Then the engine and electrical system on the boat decided to stall while they were still miles away from port. When it wouldn't restart, Bubba went to the radio to report the problem and dropped the microphone on the deck, breaking it. Since the radio was out, they weren't able to call John or any of the other boats in the fleet. Wyatt and Pierre worked on the engine, finally managing to get it running enough to get them back four hours late.

The sun had set when they pulled alongside the dock where all the boats in the Gypsy Fleet tied up. The other boats were already secured, their crews no doubt off having a beer.

Salem was still wearing her wetsuit when she stepped wearily onto the dock, a towel draped around her neck. As she passed the *Gypsy III*, one of the deckhands called out to her.

"Hey, Salem. Either you or Wyatt better get over to the boss's cottage. He's fit for bear."

Raising her hand to shield her eyes, she asked, "Why? Is something wrong?"

"That's what he wants to know. He's been calling every boat in the fleet wanting to know if we'd seen the *Two*. He wasn't at all happy when we had to report you weren't in yet."

"Did anyone contact him once we docked?"

The deckhand grinned. "Yeah. He's still not happy."

Since Wyatt had gone to get their air tanks refilled and to find a mechanic to look at the engine, it was up to her to explain to John what had happened. As she walked the rest of the way up the dock to shore, she looked around, half expecting to see John waiting. Staying on shore must be trying his patience to the limit. Their coming in late certainly wasn't going to make him jump for joy.

She would have preferred going to Delta's to shower and change first. Salt water had dried on her skin, making her feel hot and sticky. But she knew the longer John waited, the harder it would be to make him understand why they hadn't notified him of the delay.

As she walked to the cottage, Salem unzipped her wetsuit. Out on the water, the breeze had kept her cool, but now she was feeling the heat, even though the sun had set. She could remove the wetsuit altogether, but all she wore underneath was the red bikini. Her shirt and shorts were still on the boat. She debated going back for them but decided she'd better go placate John right away.

When she brought the zipper down, her fingers brushed across the Spanish coin she always wore. The gold coin was from the first treasure find John had been involved in, and she had never removed it since the day he had given it to her when she was nine years old. Then the coin on the long chain had come to her waist. Now it rested just above the cleft between her breasts.

Using one end of the towel to wipe the perspiration from her face, she approached the cottage. The exterior hadn't changed much since the previous summer. The gray shutters had received a fresh coat of paint, but the two old wicker chairs on the small front porch looked the same, their cushions faded from the sun and salty air. The large banyan tree at the side overhung the roof, its shade providing cool relief at least on that side of the cottage. Unlike Delta's house, there were few flowering shrubs.

Salem raised her hand to knock on the door, but before she could, it flew open.

John stood in the doorway, his eyes flashing green fire. Wearing jeans and a red sweatshirt with the sleeves cut off above the elbow, he glared down at her. He needed a shave and had apparently been running his fingers through his hair.

He grabbed the ends of the towel in his good hand and hauled her up on her toes until her face was inches from his. "Where in hell have you been?"

"The boat had engine trouble."

He frowned. "What kind of trouble?"

"I don't know. Pierre said it could just be that salt water got into the engine. They managed to get it going again, but we took it slow coming back. Bubba accidently broke the microphone, which is why Charlie couldn't call you on the radio."

He released her. "Why didn't Wyatt or Charlie call me when you got in? I had to hear from Wingo on the *Three* that you were back."

Feeling perspiration roll down her cheek and

neck, she raised the towel to blot her face. "I don't know, John," she said wearily. "Why don't you ask Charlie or Wyatt?"

Muttering a blunt obscenity, he pulled her into the cool interior of the cottage, shutting the door behind her. "Why are you still in your wetsuit?"

"Things were a bit hectic. Do you think I could have something cold to drink while you're yelling at me?"

He shook his head in exasperation. "I suppose." He started toward the kitchen, then halted. "Do us both a favor, Salem. Don't take off the wetsuit now. I know you're hotter than hell, but I also know what you wear underneath it. Even if your bikini was made of barbed wire, I couldn't guarantee I could keep my hands off you."

She stared after him, her heart thudding loudly at the thought of his hands skimming over her heated flesh. Shaking her head to clear it, she walked into the living room. How could he make provocative statements like that, then retreat, leaving her aching and confused?

Too restless to sit down, she stopped near the entertainment center, and turned on the radio. It was tuned to an easy-listening station, and she stood there for a few minutes before turning to gaze at the room. A sturdy wood-framed sofa and matching chairs were arranged around an enormous low table made from a slab of a cypress tree. The highly polished surface was covered with a film of dust, at least the parts of it she could see. Most of it was covered by magazines, a coffee cup, several days' worth of newspapers, and a plastic take-out container. One of Wyatt's shirts lay over the back of a chair, and a carryout pizza box sat on the floor beside it.

The condition of the living room was an indication of how much John's injuries were still bothering him. Wyatt was a slob, and John was a neatnik. Apparently, John hadn't felt like cleaning up after Wyatt when he returned to the cottage. Considering it had been three days, Salem was surprised he hadn't shoveled out the mess by now. Could his injuries be more severe than anyone was telling her?

Even though he was barefooted and made no sound when he returned from the kitchen, she knew the instant he entered the room. She raised her eyes and met his brooding gaze as he came toward her, a glass of iced tea in his hand.

She accepted the glass and raised it to her lips. Closing her eyes, she drank almost half its contents at once, soothing her dry throat. Satisfied, she kicked off her deck shoes and sat on the couch, one leg curled under her.

John stayed where he was for a moment, wondering how wise it was not to insist she leave right away. Now that he could see for himself she was all right, he should be walking her to the door. Instead, he stepped around the pizza box and sat down in the chair several feet from her. He watched her slowly roll the cool glass across her forehead, his body reacting to the bliss in her eyes.

She wore no makeup. Her dark hair was sticky with salt and tangled from the wind and water. Her lips were moist from the glass, and her skin showed the blush of a slight sunburn. In a few weeks, she would be as tanned as she had been before she went away to college. His gut clenched as he remembered how pale her breasts had been compared to the rest of her when he had removed her shirt four years ago. The memories of that night had haunted him ever since.

She rested her head on the back of the couch, closing her eyes again as she continued to touch her heated skin with the glass.

"Salem?"

"Hmmm?"

The sound vibrated along his nerve endings, reminding him of the deep throaty moan she had made when he had taken one of her breasts in his mouth four years ago. Because of the memories riding him, his voice was harsher than he intended.

"Wyatt said you weren't having any problems with the dives. I want to hear you tell me."

She slowly opened her eyes and met his gaze. Her breath caught as she recognized the heated arousal in the depths of his hazel eyes. Her body reacted instantly, her breasts becoming heavy and aching for his touch, her heartbeat accelerating painfully.

With extreme effort, she replied casually. "I'd forgotten how heavy an air tank was, but once I was in the water, it didn't matter. I was tired the first couple of days, yet aside from a little sunburn, I haven't had any problems." She smiled, the joy of diving shining in her eyes. "The first time I dove over the side, I wasn't thinking about looking for wreckage. Everything was so beautiful, so familiar."

He smiled too. "I remember when I took you down for your first scuba lesson. You kept holding your breath, even though I had taught you how to breathe into the mouthpiece."

"It wasn't because I was afraid. I had never seen

anything so wonderful. It was like entering another world. It still is."

"I know."

She heard the odd note in his voice. "I'm sorry. It must be hard for you to remain on shore while the rest of us go out."

The soft romantic background music was getting on his nerves. He rose and went over to turn off the radio. "That's part of it."

"How long do you have to have the cast on?"

He glanced down at his wrist. "Until tomorrow. I'm having this thing cut off and a temporary plastic cast put on."

"Why? Your wrist can't possibly be healed by now."

"With the plastic cast, I can go diving." He saw her lips tighten. "Don't worry. I'm not taking your place. You can still go out. There will be three of us diving."

She uncurled her leg from under her and set the glass down on the table. "Are you sure that's a good idea? What about the headaches? Wyatt said you still weren't sleeping, and he thinks it's because your head injury is bothering you."

John didn't bother to deny he was having difficulty sleeping. It was true, but it wasn't because of being hit on the head. "I'm going."

From past experiences, Salem knew he could be as stubborn as a mule and as unyielding as a brick wall. But she had to try to make him see how foolish it was for him to go diving so soon after he had been hurt.

She stood, yanking the towel from around her neck and dropping it on the sofa. "John," she said quietly, walking toward him, "please don't go diving yet." She placed her hand on his arm. "Give your wrist time to heal."

He gazed down at her. "I won't go through another day like today, not knowing what was happening. I might not be much help, but at least I'll know what the hell is going on."

She knew he must have hated feeling helpless and out of touch, not only with the boat but with her and Wyatt. She couldn't stop him. No one could once he had made up his mind.

"Wyatt can take care of himself, and you're no longer responsible for me, John. I know some habits are hard to break but . . ."

He cupped the side of her neck with his good hand, his thumb sliding under her chin so she had to raise her head. "It isn't a habit, and I don't feel responsible for you in the way you mean."

She brought her hand up to enclose his wrist. Perhaps she was being unreasonable, but he made her feel defensive. "If it was just Wyatt and the rest of the crew going out in the boat, you wouldn't be removing your cast. You would trust them to handle whatever problems came up."

"Let's leave Wyatt out of this," he said roughly. Suddenly needing to erase the painful memory of Wyatt holding Salem in his arms, as he had the other night at Delta's, John lowered his head and kissed her.

Salem didn't resist. All she could do was respond. She was swept away into the wondrous world of passion that only John could take her to. It was like being engulfed in a current stronger than any surge of water she'd felt in the ocean.

John tasted the salt on her skin, and his body hardened as he thought of how the rest of her would taste. Holding her firmly against him with his encasted arm, he ignored the pain in his wrist. The agony of wanting her was much worse.

His left hand lowered the wetsuit's zipper to her waist, giving him access to the moist skin beneath. His fingers found their way under her brief top until her breast filled his hand. The soft yearning sound deep in her throat drove his control to the limit. He raised his head enough to look down at her.

"This isn't habit," he muttered. "This is madness."

She stared at him, eyes glazed with torrid passion, then shook her head. "No." Her voice was low and sultry. "This is us."

The cast rubbed roughly over the rubber suit as he pressed her hips to his. He sucked in his breath when she arched her back, bringing her lower body more tightly against him.

"Don't, Salem. I'm barely hanging on as it is."

She saw the tortured look in his eyes. Feeling as though she had been doused with ice-cold water, she realized nothing had changed after all. His body wanted her in the most basic way. His mind still resisted her.

She lowered her arms, her hands falling heavily to her sides. Defeat lay like a lead weight on her heart. How could he think something so wonderful could be so wrong? she wondered for about the hundredth time. She couldn't fight an unknown enemy, and he was never going to tell her the name of her opponent.

Taking a step back, she broke away from his grasp. "All right," she said hoarsely.

He frowned. "All right what?"

She took a deep breath, hoping to cool her heated blood. "I thought I was strong enough to take anything you handed out when I came back. I'm not. One minute you make me feel as though I'm the only woman in the world for you. Then you push me away as though I'm something unclean you can't bear to touch."

Shock arced through him. "Salem," he said in a raw voice. "You've got it all wrong."

Her mouth twisted in a mirthless smile. "Obviously. I've been wrong all along, haven't I? I thought we had something special between us. I didn't realize the only response I created in you was purely sexual, a man lusting after a woman. Well, you can relax. I've learned my lesson."

She turned abruptly and wrenched open the door, leaving before she made an even bigger fool of herself.

Four

Once she was out of sight of the cottage, Salem slowed her pace. Without thinking about where she was going, she retraced her steps to the dock area. The pavement under her bare feet was still warm from the rays of the sun, making her realize she had left her deck shoes at the cottage.

It wasn't all she had left behind. Her pride seemed to have been misplaced there as well.

She couldn't bear to face Delta or Connie yet. With their sharp eyes, they'd immediately see she was upset, and she wasn't up to putting on a false front. She needed to be alone for a while to pull herself together. If such a thing was possible. Knowing the two women would worry if she didn't come home, she wished she had some money so she could call them from a pay phone. But she didn't, so she'd just take the time she needed to sort herself out. When she was calmer, she would go back to the house.

Since going to Delta's was out of the question, she chose another place where she could have privacy. Her home away from home. The Gypsy Fleet.

When she reached the dock, she saw one of the deckhands sitting on an overturned keg enjoying a cigar. There didn't appear to be anyone else around. She had forgotten that John had arranged to have one of the crew on guard at the docks every night as a precaution. Though there were lights about every ten feet, high up on poles, on both sides of the wooden dock, the boats were all dark. She saw no other crew members around. Apparently, Wyatt and the mechanic were through working on the engine on the *Gypsy II*.

The deckhand recognized her as she approached. "Good evening, Salem," he said with surprise, his eyes full of curiosity. "Did you forget something?"

"Hi, Wingo," she replied. "I'll be on the *Two* for a few minutes. Then I'm going on *Gypsy One* for a couple of hours."

She could tell by his expression he thought her behavior was odd, but thankfully he didn't ask any further questions. He shrugged, mumbled "Okay," and returned to his cigar.

Aboard the *II*, she retrieved the shirt and shorts she had worn earlier. The broken microphone had been replaced, and the engine hatch had been secured, so apparently Wyatt had been busy. For all his outward careless attitude, he always managed to get things done efficiently and quickly.

Leaving the boat, she crossed the dock and climbed aboard the older *Gypsy I*, the boat John had bought after he had received his share of the treasure almost fifteen years ago. She had always preferred this one to the newer, more modern boats in the fleet. She had learned to cook on the small galley stove, had scrubbed its teak decks, and had gone out daily, baiting hooks for the tourists who had paid to be taken fishing.

Now she appreciated the old boat because it had a shower. Stepping down into the cabin, she flicked the light switch on. Since the boat had been tied up to the dock while repairs were being made, she hoped the crew had kept the fresh-water tank filled. A few minutes later, she was relieved when cool water sprayed from the small shower attachment. She quickly peeled off the wetsuit and her drenched bikini, and stepped into the tiny cubicle. The clean fresh water felt heavenly, but because the supply was limited, she washed her hair and body quickly, then rinsed the salt water off her wetsuit.

After drying with the only towel she could find, she slipped on her shirt and shorts. Running her fingers through her wet hair was the best she could do for it since she didn't have a comb with her. It didn't matter. There was no one to see her, and she didn't particularly care how she looked at the moment.

Once she was dressed, she had nothing to occupy her mind, and the pain rushed back as the scene in John's cottage replayed itself in detail. She wrapped her arms around her middle and sank down on one of the berths. As she rocked back and forth, a soft tortured moan rose from her throat. Her eyes burned, but she refused to give in to the need to cry out the anguish coiled tightly around her heart.

Just because she loved John didn't mean he had to love her back. He might be attracted to her, but it was obvious by his actions that he didn't want to be. She kept insisting she was an adult now. It was time to behave like one, rather than a spoiled child who couldn't have what she so badly wanted. If only John had continued to be cold toward her, she might have been able to accept the situation sooner. Yet each kiss, each touch of his hands, fed her hopes. And each time he pushed her away, the rejection was more painful than the last.

Still clutching her middle, she collapsed on the berth, letting the gentle rocking of the boat soothe her. Rolling onto her side, she closed her eyes. Somehow she was going to have to accept that John was not going to change his mind.

Or she would have to leave Key West.

A little after eleven that night Wyatt drove down to the docks. Out of habit, he was going to check on the boats before he went home. The scent of Cheryl's perfume still lingered on his skin, and he smiled to himself. She had been a little miffed when he was late picking her up for their dinner date, but after he had explained why, she had forgiven him. As the daughter of a fisherman, Cheryl knew all about the various problems that could come up on the sea. She hadn't even objected to the somewhat disreputable jeans and knit shirt he'd been wearing, the odor of salt water and diesel oil clinging to them.

He'd had it with possessive women, especially after that episode with Maria a couple of months ago. With some women, it didn't pay even to buy them a drink. She'd taken the simple social offer and made it into an invitation for something more serious. Since then, she'd appeared at his table in restaurants when he was with another woman, phoned the cottage at all hours, and waited on the dock for him to return. When tact hadn't worked, he'd been blunt, telling her he was sorry she had misunderstood his intentions. He wasn't interested in her. He hadn't enjoyed telling her that or the sight of her tears, but it had been necessary.

Humming the last song he and Cheryl had danced to at the Havana Docks Bar, he decided he might break his own limit of dating a woman no more than three times. Cheryl was good company, undemanding, and she wasn't possessive. He wasn't looking for a long-term relationship, and apparently neither was she.

His complacent smile was replaced by a frown when he saw a light showing through the porthole in the *Gyspy I*. He parked his Jeep near the entrance to the dock and got out. Wingo had been replaced by Sandy, an older man who had been working for the fleet for four years. Scuttlebutt had it that Sandy had once been the captain of a large cruise ship that had run aground while he was in command. John hadn't cared about the rumors, judging the man on the work he did for the fleet.

When Wyatt approached him, Sandy was knocking his pipe against the dock post next to the keg he was sitting on. He looked up, nodding when he recognized Wyatt.

"Who's on the *One*, Sandy?"

"Wingo said Miss Salem went aboard earlier tonight."

Wyatt's eyes narrowed as he looked from Sandy to the boat behind him. "Salem? What's she doing there?"

Sandy shrugged. "I don't know. Figured it was her business and none of mine."

"Is she alone?"

Refilling his pipe from the pouch he had taken out of his shirt pocket, Sandy muttered, "Far as I know."

Puzzled, Wyatt started walking toward the old boat, his long strides eating up the distance. Once aboard, he stepped down into the cabin. He was about to call her name when he saw Salem curled up on the port berth. She was asleep.

He noticed her wetsuit was lying on the narrow counter, along with her bikini. The clothes she was wearing were the same ones she'd had on when he picked her up at Delta's that morning. Her hair was still damp, which indicated she had taken a shower on the boat.

For a moment, he debated letting her sleep, then decided to wake her so he could take her home.

Touching her shoulder, he gently nudged her. "Salem. Wake up, sugar. It's time little girls were safely tucked into their beds."

He shook her a little harder and saw her dark lashes slowly raise. It took a few seconds for her to focus, and her expression was wary until she realized who had awakened her.

"What time is it?" she asked drowsily.

"About eleven-thirty. What are you doing sleeping on the boat?"

Her expression changed abruptly, and he was startled to see haunted shadows darken her eyes.

He sat down on the edge of the bed and stroked her back. "What's going on, brat?"

Feeling defenseless lying down, Salem sat up, wrapping her arms around her drawn-up legs. "I shouldn't have come back."

The hollow sound of her voice was so unlike

her, Wyatt pressed her for more information. "Why not?"

She looked out the porthole rather than meet his curious eyes. "It's too hard."

"The diving? If I've been pushing you too much, why didn't you say so?"

She shook her head. "It's not the diving." She turned to look at him. "It's John."

A look of comprehension crossed Wyatt's face. "Have you had another fight?"

She didn't answer, not wanting to go over the details, even with Wyatt. "Why does he hate me, Wyatt?"

He stared at her, obviously shocked. Then he laughed. "Good Lord, Salem. The man doesn't hate you. He loves you. He always has."

Her smile was ragged around the edges. "Like a big brother?" She sighed heavily and leaned back against the bulkhead. "You've always loved me, too, Wyatt. That isn't the kind of love I want from John." She paused, hating to admit the truth. "I've made a big fool of myself. I don't think of him as my big brother, and I've made it obvious."

Wyatt put his arm around her and drew her head to his shoulder. "From what I've seen, making a fool of yourself is part of being in love. Which is why I'm staying the hell out of it. But you're wrong about John's feelings, Salem. I've had to put up with his bad moods for six years because of you."

She wanted to believe him, but she couldn't. "I've only been gone four years."

He chuckled. "It started when you were sixteen. I can even give you the time and the place. It was a week after your sixteenth birthday. It was one of the busiest seasons we'd had and we had just ought the *Gypsy Two*. You'd been working in Delta's gallery most of the summer and hadn't been out diving for some time. You went out with us the day we tried out the new boat. We all went diving, and when we returned to the boat, John reached down to help you up, as one of us usually did. Because we didn't plan to stay in the water long, none of us had worn wetsuits. You were wearing that skimpy yellow thing Delta had bought you for your birthday. One of your flippers tripped you up, and you stumbled against him. You obviously didn't see his face. He looked like someone had punched him in the gut."

She tilted her head back, frowning up at Wyatt. "I've practically lived in a bikini ever since I was eight years old."

He smiled wryly. "At sixteen, you . . . ah, didn't have the figure of an eight-year-old. John noticed. I think it's the first time he realized you had . . . uh, filled out. He's been like a bear with a thorn in his paw ever since. You're the thorn. He can't remove it, so he tries to live with the irritation."

Salem straightened up. "He effectively removed me by sending me away to college."

Wyatt gave a martyred sigh. "That only made it worse. There were times I would have gladly pushed him over the side and left him out in the Gulf. I wish you two would stop fighting each other. It would certainly make my life a helluva lot easier."

"You're wrong about how John feels about me. He might want me sexually, but that's all."

Wyatt coughed as though he suddenly had something caught in his throat. After a moment he said in a strained voice, "I'm not sure this is a subject we should be discussing, brat. Unlike

John, I still think of you as my little sister, and talking about your sex life is disconcerting."

Salem looked at him closely. Wyatt Brodie was embarrassed! She had thought there was nothing on earth that could rattle him. For the first time since she had left the cottage, she smiled. "Relax. There's nothing to talk about."

"I figured that out for myself. Otherwise, John wouldn't be so damned grumpy."

She knew she wasn't being fair, but she asked a question she'd wondered about for a long time. "Has John been with other women while I've been gone?"

Wyatt held up his hand as though pushing the question away. "Oh, no. I'm not getting in the middle of this. That's something you should be asking John. On second thought, maybe you'd better not." He pushed himself up. "Come on. I'll walk you back to Delta's. A good night's sleep, and you'll be back to driving John crazy. Who knows? Maybe one of these days, he'll stop fighting the inevitable."

She shook her head. "I'm going to stay here for a while longer. Would you call Delta in her studio and tell her I'm all right, that I'll be home later?"

He put his hands on his slim hips, just as John did when he was annoyed. "You can't sit here sulking, Salem. For one thing, it won't accomplish anything, and for another, it's not safe. If the Porto brothers plan another attack on the boats, you could be hurt."

"I won't be here much longer. I'm just not ready to go home yet. Besides, there's a guard watching the boats."

The rude sound Wyatt made deep in his throat was an indication of how he felt about Sandy's abilities as a guard. "He's only one man. He's watching the shore. The Portos could come in by boat just as easily." He saw the defiant tilt of her chin and muttered, "Hell, I don't know who's more stubborn, you or John. No wonder you're making life miserable for each other. And me."

Salem watched him stomp up the steps, then heard his footsteps cross the teak deck. After a moment she heard nothing but the gentle slap of water against the boat. The night air had seeped into the cabin, and she rubbed her arms to warm them.

It would have made more sense to go back to the house with Wyatt, but nothing she'd done all evening had made much sense. Why start now? she asked herself as she rummaged in one of the lockers for something to ward off the chill. She found a thick black cotton sweater that she remembered John wearing years ago. One sleeve had a ragged hole in the elbow, and the sweater smelled like a musty attic, but it was warm. When she pulled it on over her head, the hem fell to her thighs and the sleeves covered her hands. Shoving up the cuffs, she shut off the intrusive light and returned to the berth. Even though she hadn't eaten all day, she didn't bother looking through the cupboards for food. Chances were good there wouldn't be anything remotely edible anyway. She positioned herself so she could look out the porthole, although there wasn't a great deal she could see except the moonlight glittering on the water.

She had to figure out what she was going to do. Hopefully, she would come up with the answer before morning.

*   *   *

When Wyatt walked up the path toward the cottage, he saw no lights inside. It figured, he thought. The one night he wanted to talk to John, and John had finally managed to get some sleep. He didn't realize John was sitting in one of the wicker chairs on the front porch until he started to slip his house key into the lock.

"It's open."

Startled, Wyatt dropped the keys. "Dammit, John. A man can only take so many shocks in one day."

"Getting jumpy in your old age?"

"Apparently."

Wyatt fumbled around for his keys, found them, and shoved them into his pocket. As though the weight of the world were on his shoulders, he flopped down on the sagging cushion of the other chair, then gladly accepted the cold bottle of beer John handed him.

"Have you been working on the engine all this time?" John asked.

Wyatt took a long pull on the bottle before answering. "That only took a half hour. It was a loose wire, but the mechanic had trouble finding it. It made me a little late for my date with Cheryl, then—"

"Cheryl? Why would you be out with Cheryl?"

Wyatt's brows rose at the strange question. "Why not? She's single, over twenty-one, and pleasant to look at. I think that blow on the head must have jarred something loose, John. You haven't quizzed me about my dates since I was fifteen and you gave me that fascinating lecture on the birds and the bees and being responsible. Why now?"

Irritated that he had to point out the obvious, John spoke harshly. "Because Salem is back."

"So?"

Fury replaced irritation. Wyatt's blunt question grated against his raw nerves. "Delta phoned several hours ago. She said Salem hadn't come home yet and wanted to know if she was here. I figured she was with you."

"Why would you figure that?"

"I know how you feel about Salem, Wyatt. I know you're past the age when I can tell you what to do, but I would hate to see Salem hurt."

"So quit hurting her."

John jerked his head around to stare at Wyatt's shadowy profile. "Me? You're the one seeing other women."

Wyatt didn't answer immediately, as though he needed time to rally his thoughts. "Let me get this straight," he murmured finally. "You think I'm interested in Salem romantically? Is that what all this is about?"

John left the chair and strode over to one of the porch posts. His fingers clenched on the wood. "I've seen you two together. I heard your voice when you called her when she was in school. You care about her."

"Of course I care about her," Wyatt said, his voice revealing his bewilderment that he had to explain something that should be crystal clear. "She's the sister I never had, a friend, someone I would trust with my life. Good Lord, John. Is this why you're treating Salem so badly? You think I'm in love with her?"

John felt the year-old knot of tension loosen

deep inside him, but he still needed everything clarified. "You were always calling her when she was in college. And when she was home, you two were together a great deal. I saw you the other night at Delta's. You were holding her."

"I was comforting her, you big bozo, because she was upset with you. I called her because I missed her. She spent time with me when she came home because I enjoy her company." Wyatt stood and walked over to John. "I love Salem, but I'm not in love with her. There's a big difference. I appreciate the fact that you were willing to step aside because you thought I wanted Salem, but it's not necessary. We've gone past the stage when you have to make sacrifices for me and Salem, John. If you care about her as deeply as I'm beginning to think you do, then do something about it. She's on the *Gypsy One*."

John turned in surprise. "What's she doing there?"

"Trying to figure out why you hate her." When John gaped at him as though he had lost his mind, Wyatt added dryly, "You've given me a lot of advice over the years, good advice that's been a great help to me, but when it comes to women, I'll muddle through on my own. You might know a lot about what makes a boat tick, but not women."

Feeling as though a heavy weight had been lifted from his heart, John smiled faintly. "I think you're right."

"So what are you waiting for?" Wyatt asked, amusement and affection in his voice. "Go to her and straighten out the mess you've made. Then maybe we can all get back to normal."

"Give me the keys to your Jeep. You're parked behind mine."

Wyatt dug into his pocket and handed John the keys. "I won't wait up."

John laid his hand on Wyatt's shoulder. "Thanks. And I don't mean for the keys."

Wyatt nodded, then jerked his head in the direction of the Jeep. "Anytime. Now go to her."

Sandy was at the end of the dock, shining a flashlight around the boat tied up there when John arrived. Seeing John, he strolled back up the dock.

John met him halfway, stopping near the *Gypsy I*. "Is everything all right?"

The older man shrugged. "I thought I heard a noise like oars in the water, but I didn't see anything."

"Wyatt said Salem was aboard the *One*, but there aren't any lights on. Is she still there?"

"She hasn't left as far as I know."

"I'll be on the *One* if something comes up."

Sandy nodded, then headed back toward the entrance to the dock without asking any questions.

Once aboard, John stepped down into the cabin. He flicked on the light above the galley sink, which gave enough lumination for him to see his way into the aft berthing space. In the dim shadows, he could make out Salem's slender form on the port berth. She was lying on her side facing him, her upper body wrapped in an old black sweater he thought had been lost a long time ago. His soft-soled shoes made little sound as he slowly walked over to her.

The mattress was a thick pad covering the

built-in bunk, and it didn't give when he sat down near her hip. Now that he was with her, the urgency to clear up the problems between them didn't seem as important. It was enough just to be near her. Her breathing was slow and deep, her lashes dark against her tanned cheek. In sleep she looked vulnerable and lovely. The little gypsy girl had become a beautiful woman. His woman.

As badly as he wanted to touch her, he needed time to let it sink in that there were no longer any barriers between them. He was free to love her without the agony of thinking Wyatt also wanted her. And it had been agony to have his heart torn apart by the two people he loved so deeply. A little while ago Wyatt had said it was no longer necessary for him to sacrifice his own needs for them. He'd never thought of it in those terms before. When he had taken them away from the orphanage, he had vowed to make them happy. He hadn't realized he had still been doing it, considering their needs more important than his.

Wyatt's blunt assessment of the situation had broken the chains of responsibility. They were adults now, free to choose their own ways.

He raised his hand to brush a lock of hair away from Salem's cheek. Now all he had to do was convince her he had been a fool. He smiled as he stared down at her. Somehow he didn't think that was going to be too difficult.

Touching her was no longer enough. He needed to feel her next to him, to soothe the ache he'd had for so long. Kicking off his shoes, he turned on his side and lay down beside her. The single berth wasn't wide, and since she was in the mid-

dle of it, there wasn't much room for his large
frame.

Propping himself up on his elbow, he pressed
his lower body against hers to shift her over a
little.

She made a low grumbling sound and started
to roll over onto her other side, but he stopped
her with a hand on her waist. "No. Stay here so
I can see you."

Her breathing caught, then quickened, but her
eyes remained closed. "Don't wake me up." Her
words were slurred and spoken so softly, he had
to bend down to hear them. "I'm having a lovely
dream."

His hands slipped beneath the bulky sweater,
then under her shirt. Her body was warm, her
skin satiny. "What are you dreaming about?" he
whispered.

"You touching me like you did four years ago."

He hesitated, still not sure. "Who's touching
you?"

Her brow creased in a frown, then his name
came out on a gentle sigh. "John."

His heart beat hard. Sliding his hand up her
rib cage, he found her bare breast. Even half
asleep, she reacted to his touch, pressing against
his hand.

He lowered his head to taste her lips, but he
needed more, much more. "Open your eyes,
Salem."

Though his body blocked out most of the light,
he could see her lashes slowly raise to reveal
drowsy blue-gray eyes. She parted her lips in
surprise.

"Am I still dreaming?"

"If you are, then I'm dreaming the same dream."

Needing to assure herself he was really there with her, she lifted a hand and pressed it against his cheek. "In my dream," she murmured huskily, "you didn't need a shave."

He smiled. "In my dreams you aren't wearing a smelly old sweater. In fact, you aren't wearing anything at all."

Drowsiness was replaced by awareness, then a guarded wariness. "No," she said, unable to keep her pain out of her voice. She dropped her hand to his chest. "It hurts too much when you push me away."

"I'm not going to push you away ever again, Salem."

She closed her eyes as his large hand kneaded her breast, his thumb stroking the tip. This had to be a dream, she thought. If it was, she never wanted to wake up.

She felt his lips against hers, felt his warm breath as he murmured, "Open your eyes, sweetheart. I want to see how they change when I touch you."

Obeying his command, she raised her lashes. She would do anything he asked as long as he didn't stop what he was doing. "What changed your mind, John? Several hours ago, you were telling me there wasn't a chance for anything between us."

"Later," he whispered against her throat. "We'll talk later. Right now I want to just hold you, taste you."

Salem knew she should insist they talk now, but it was so wonderful to be in his arms. It was so much like her dream, she wanted to hold on to the delicious sensations and never let go of them.

Five

This time when he kissed her, John held nothing back. All restraints had been snapped by the knowledge that there was no longer a reason he had to resist her. Slanting his mouth over hers, he drank deeply. He was acutely aware of every sound she made, every breath she took, every movement of her fingers in his hair.

Enjoying the luscious feel of her flesh, he was no longer satisfied with caressing only her breast. His hand slid down to the fastening of her shorts, and he felt her stomach tighten as his knuckles brushed against her skin. She was so hot, so soft, like satin would feel after it was left out in the sunlight. He shuddered as her arms came around him, her slender length pressed against him.

With the barrier removed from his mind, he wanted the obstacle of their clothing gone too. But he didn't want to rush her or himself. Instead he gave his hands and lips the freedom he had never allowed before. If she rejected him, he wouldn't blame her, but she didn't. Nor did she only receive his caresses. She gave as well. Her body trembled against his as her hands stroked his back and shoulders, her lips clung to his.

When he broke the kiss so he could tug the sweater over her head, she made a sound of impatience. Throwing the sweater to the floor, he began to unbutton her shirt, gently pushing her on her back. Parting the material, he gazed avidly at her breasts, letting his eyes feast on her.

"I've never told you how beautiful you are," he whispered, "how you take my breath away whether you're wearing that red dress or these ragged clothes." His hand slid over her hip beneath the loosened shorts. "The charming child has grown up to become an exciting woman."

He was saying all the wonderful things she had always wanted to hear, Salem thought, gazing up at him. So why was she still holding back her enjoyment of being in his arms? Maybe he could forget everything that had happened between them in the past. For her, it wasn't that easy. His last rejection was still an open wound, healed partially by his caresses but not completely.

Although he wasn't able to see her eyes clearly in the shadows, John sensed her wariness. He couldn't blame her. His hot-and-cold treatment of her in the past didn't give her any reason to believe tonight would be different.

Sliding his hand out from under her shorts, he brushed a few tendrils of hair from her face. "I know I've hurt you in the past, Salem. Sometimes I had to touch you. Then I hated myself for giving in to that need when I thought it was wrong."

Emotion tightened her throat, making her voice hoarse and shaky. "A few hours ago, you still felt it was wrong. What changed your mind?"

"I talked to Wyatt."

She gave him a blank look. "I don't understand. Why would talking to Wyatt make any difference?"

"I thought Wyatt wanted you." He saw her eyes widen in genuine shock. "I was trying to be noble by stepping aside, since I thought you cared about him too. You always seemed more at ease with him than with me. You went into Wyatt's arms often, like the other night in the kitchen at Delta's. He phoned you regularly while you were at school. He often mentioned how much he missed you." He stroked the back of his fingers along her jawline. "I could share the business, the cottage, and just about everything else in my life with Wyatt, but not you."

Remembering what he had said in Seattle about her not knowing who she was, she said quietly, "Maybe you wanted to believe I was involved with Wyatt. It made it easier for you to send me away."

"Easy?" he growled. "Sending you to college was the hardest thing I ever had to do. Dammit, Salem. You were only eighteen, just beginning to experience the emotions of a woman. I was your guardian. I've been like a father figure to you since you were eight years old. When I saw you with Wyatt, then saw the way you reacted to me, I thought it was better for everyone if you went away to get an education and to grow up. It tore me apart to make you go, but I still think it was the best thing for you."

"I thought you knew me better than anyone else in the world, but you don't really know me at all, do you?"

The anger in her voice baffled him. "Why do you say that?"

"Did you really think I could melt in your arms, want to make love with you, then go to Wyatt?"

Her words conjured up pictures in his mind that he'd had to live with for four years. He didn't like them any better now than then, even though he knew there was no basis for them.

"I didn't know what to think. I admit I was having trouble adjusting to the change in our relationship. It was hard to live with the fact that I wanted to make love to my ward, the little girl I had stolen out of the orphanage and taken care of for so many years."

Surprising both of them, Salem closed her fingers around his wrist and brought his hand down to her naked breast. "I'm not a little girl any longer, John."

He gazed at his hand covering her breast, and fire stirred deep within him. "I know," he said hoarsely. "That's been a big part of the problem."

Before they went any further, Salem needed to make one last thing clear. If he was to accept her, it had to be on equal terms. "I'm not dependent on you any longer. I can support myself, manage my own life, and survive without your assistance if I have to." She pressed down on the back of his hand, pleased when he clasped her aching flesh. "But I don't want to have to do without this magic I feel when you touch me."

Lowering his head, he murmured her name against her mouth. His whole body burned with the need to bury himself deep inside her. He had wanted her for so long. The craving had become a constant companion, riding him during long lonely days and haunting his empty dark nights.

Her hand fumbled at the snap of his jeans, and he sucked in his breath as a shaft of heat seared him. He lifted his head to watch her eyes as he covered her hand with his, moving it lower. Her eyes darkened, desire stirring in their depths, when he pressed her hand over the hard ridge beneath his jeans. Then he felt her fingers clasp him, and he couldn't hold back a hoarse groan of pleasure.

A small section of his mind that could still think rationally urged him to ask the question that had been nagging at him for a long time. "Salem, have you ever been with a man before?"

She felt a pang of regret that he could imagine she would want to be with any man but him. "No."

He closed his eyes. It wouldn't have made any difference, but he was glad he would be the first. As his hands swept over her, he knew he also wanted to be the last, the only man she ever knew intimately. Opening his eyes, he met her gaze.

"I've wanted you for a long time, Salem. I can't keep kissing you and feeling you against me without making love to you. Tell me what you want."

That was easy. "You."

Pushing her shirt from her shoulders, he slid his arm under her to raise her. If the strain on his broken wrist caused him pain, he was unaware of it. He was aware only of other sensations, sharp darts of pleasure as he tasted first one breast then the other. Intense satisfaction flowed through him as she melted against him.

Her legs lifted to cradle him, and she arched her hips into his, pressing against her hand that was still holding him captive. Nearly mindless with desire, he managed to lace his fingers through hers, lingering for a moment before he brought her hand away from his aching body.

His tongue forged deeply into her mouth. If she

was aware of him tugging her shorts down her legs, she gave no indication of it. Only when he pushed away from her to strip off his own clothes did she make a sound of protest. As he undressed, he could feel her gaze on him, flowing over his chest, his waist, his hips. There was no fear or apprehension in her eyes as she gazed at his aroused body, only desire. For a moment he stared down at her, his body throbbing as though she were again touching him with her hand, not just her eyes.

Her gaze shifted to the golden coin nestled in the curling hair covering his chest. Then she raised her hand to him, a silent invitation to join her. Linking his fingers with hers, he lay back down beside her, partially covering her. She grasped his head so she could look directly at him, her eyes serious.

"I've been so empty for so long, John. Make the emptiness go away. Fill me."

Her soft words broke the bonds of his restraint. All he could manage was to groan her name as he parted her legs and eased between them. When he felt her moist heat waiting for him, he thought he would explode with the need to be inside her. Using every ounce of control he could summon, he slowly began to fill her, his eyes watching hers for any sign of discomfort.

Salem felt his arms tremble as he braced himself over her, and she knew he was holding back because of her inexperience. It wasn't what she wanted. She wanted him deep inside her, as close as two people could ever be. Sliding her hands over his muscular back, she clasped his hips and brought him forward as she raised her own hips.

He made a choked sound of pleasure as he filled

her completely, taking her mouth with the same intensity. If there was pain, she didn't feel it. If there had been a storm threatening them, she wouldn't have been aware of it. He was her world, her life, now a part of her. And it was right that they should come together on a boat, the scent of the sea blending with the magic between them.

He began to move within her, and she spun off into the sensual world he was creating for her. Instinctively she joined him in the race to find the ultimate pleasure waiting for them.

Tension coiled while passion danced. Exquisite tenderness blended with sensuality as John held her tightly. Suddenly she was swallowed up by a rippling explosion. So immersed was she in the sweet, fierce storm, she barely realized when John surged into her one more time, joining her as the world shattered around them.

A long time passed before their breathing slowed. The air was cool, but their bodies were still warm. His weight crushed her into the thin mattress, but she didn't want him to move.

John took a deep shuddering breath and raised his head. She smiled, and he saw feminine satisfaction glowing in the depths of her eyes. He had tried to be gentle with her, but when he'd felt her velvet heat surround him, he'd forgotten everything but her.

Bracing his body on his elbows, he flinched as pain arced up his arm from his broken wrist. "Are you all right?"

"Yes. But you aren't. You've hurt your wrist, haven't you?"

A corner of his mouth lifted in a smile. "It doesn't matter. If I had two broken arms and both legs in a cast, I would still have found a way to make love to you." He started to roll off her, but her arms tightened around his neck. "Salem, I'm too heavy for you."

Lifting her head, she touched his mouth with her moist lips. "When you've wanted something wonderful for a long time and it's finally given to you, you don't want to let go of it."

His smile widened, a look of male triumph in his eyes. "My gypsy has turned into a greedy woman."

She relaxed her arms. "I think you're right."

He kissed her, then withdrew from her to lie on his side, bringing her with him so she was facing him. "I'm not complaining, as long as I'm the only one you want."

Her fingers played with the gold coin around his neck as she thought about what he had said. She wanted to think he had made a commitment of sorts, yet he could simply have made a possessive statement. There had been no words of love from either of them, only the act of love. Now in the aftermath of his lovemaking, with him close beside her, it was enough. Maybe later it wouldn't be.

Copying her, he lifted the coin she wore, which had fallen over one breast. "When you came into the bar in Seattle wearing that red dress, I actually envied this coin. It was closer to you than I was able to be. I wanted my hand to be between your breasts where this coin rested. It sleeps with you, takes a shower with you, and lies against your skin wherever you go."

"Wearing the coin makes me feel closer to you. I've never taken it off."

His fingers brushed against her breast, and he could feel her skin cooling in the night air. The wool blanket covering the berth was scratchy. As much as he would have preferred to remain in bed with her, this wasn't the place for either of them to be very comfortable.

He remembered what he had said to her earlier that evening. No, the need to take care of her wasn't a habit. It was a necessity.

Scooping her up in his arms, he ignored the strain on his wrist as he carried her to the closet-sized shower. He set her down and turned on the faucet, then stepped in, snaking an arm around her waist to bring her with him.

"Your cast," she gasped in alarm.

He placed his hand high against the wall, his cast out of the streaming water, his other hand resting on the enticing curve of her hip. "Remind me to put in a hot-water heater on this boat," he muttered.

She shivered, but it had nothing to do with the cool water sluicing over her. There was barely enough room for one in the stall, and his body was pressed against hers, his skin slick and inviting.

"There isn't much water in the tank," she said. "I took a shower earlier."

John barely heard what she said. Her nearness ignited the flames of desire, stronger and even more compelling than before. Lowering his head, he took her mouth hungrily, demanding and receiving a response as immediate and powerful as his own.

Neither noticed when the stream of water slowed to a trickle, then stopped. He broke away from her to bury his lips against her throat. Her head fell back, her eyes closed as she absorbed the tremors of awakening need.

Through the haze of passion, John managed to remember her inexperience. As badly as he wanted to sheath himself deep within her, he couldn't abuse her. He lifted his head and gazed down at her, smiling when he saw the look of dazed arousal in her eyes.

He reached behind her and turned off the faucet, then opened the door and let her go ahead of him. She picked up the still-damp towel she had used earlier and swiftly dried herself.

Smiling seductively, she turned and stroked the towel over his chest. A sense of feminine power rushed over her when she heard his breathing halt, then quicken.

Returning her smile, he took the towel from her. "Salem, behave. As much as I would like to make love to you again, your body needs time to adjust." She pouted with innocent allure, and hot desire flared through him. "Let's get you back to Delta's before she calls out the National Guard."

He bent down to pick up their discarded clothing, handing hers over to her once he'd sorted them out. His eyes darkened as he watched her pull on her shorts and shirt with no undergarments. It was definitely time to take her back to Delta's. Knowing she was naked under her clothes was going to drive him crazy.

She gathered up her bathing suit and wetsuit, clutching them in her hands as she followed him up the steps. A strong breeze off the Gulf tousled her hair as she joined him on the upper deck. When he didn't make any move to leave the boat, she looked up at him. His expression of longing told her he was as reluctant to leave the privacy of the boat as she was.

His hand cupped the back of her neck. He bent down to kiss—

Suddenly a deafening explosion rent the air around them.

Six

John clamped his arms around her and brought her down with him to the deck. Pieces of wood and debris rained over them, and the boat rocked violently with the force of the blast. A second explosion as loud as the first sent more fragments flying through the air.

Salem barely had time to accept his crushing weight before he was lifting himself off her.

"Stay down," he ordered.

Then he was gone.

Raising her head, all she could see were flames rising high in the air. They were coming from the direction of the building John had built to store their diving equipment and various engine parts. Her head was still ringing with the noise from the explosions, but she could hear the crackle of the fire, the roar of the flames.

Slowly she stood up, her gaze fixed on the fire biting into the dark sky overhead. It was hard to see anything but the bright orange glow, but she strained to glimpse John. Fear clenched in a tight fist around her heart at the thought of his being in danger.

In the distance she heard the wail of sirens as the fire department and police rushed to the scene. But she could see the building was completely engulfed in flames, too far gone to be salvaged by fire hoses.

Disregarding John's order to stay on the boat, Salem jumped down onto the dock and ran the length of it. As she neared the entrance, she saw people beginning to gather, standing in bunches at a safe distance from the fire. She had no idea what time it was, other than it was late. Some of the curious onlookers wore robes over their nightwear; others were dressed in an odd assortment of clothing apparently grabbed in haste.

She didn't see any sign of Sandy as she reached the shore. Apparently, he had gone with John. She gazed around the area surrounding the shed, but it was impossible to find John among the firemen, policemen, and fire-fighting equipment.

She had to find him, had to make sure he was all right. Knowing how possessive John was of his property, she could easily imagine him rushing to save whatever he could without considering he could be hurt.

Disregarding the impatient looks she received, she pushed through several rows of people. Several yards from the shed, a yellow band of plastic had already been set up to cordon off the area. She started to duck under it, but a police officer blocked her with his arm.

"Hold it, lady. Stay behind the line."

"I need to find someone."

"You'll have to find 'em later. Stay behind the line."

Salem was debating finding another place to slip through when she heard Wyatt's voice behind the policeman. "It's all right, officer. She's one of the owners. I'll be responsible for her."

It was obvious from the policeman's expression that he didn't like to back down, but he lowered his arm and Salem sprang forward. When she reached Wyatt, she grabbed the front of his shirt. "Where's John?"

His hands came up to hold hers. "He's all right." Jerking his head toward the large fire engine, he added, "He's talking to the fire captain."

Relief washed over her, and she slumped against Wyatt. He put his arm around her shoulders and drew her away from the crowds. Now that she was closer, she could see that the walls of the building had collapsed. Powerful streams of water were aimed at the remainder of the building, and the flames were gradually losing their strength.

"How did it happen?" she asked.

"That's what John is trying to find out now." Anger simmered in Wyatt's voice. "I have an idea of my own."

She looked up at him. "The Porto brothers again?"

"A fire inspector went through that building two weeks ago with a fine-tooth comb without finding any code violations. You know how strict John is about safety, especially with the oil and diesel fuel stored there. The inspector probably didn't even find a grease rag lying around. The building couldn't have exploded on its own."

"First the attack on John and the crewmen, now this," she mused aloud.

"There have been a couple of other incidents, but none as serious as this one. We're going to have to do something before someone ends up getting killed. We can't just wait around for something else to happen."

As they neared the fire engine, Salem was finally able to see John. The tight knot of fear for his safety loosened in her chest. He was talking to a man wearing a fireman's yellow protective coat. His face was smudged, his cast streaked with soot.

As though he had heard her call his name, he looked around. When he saw her, his expression became furious. Abruptly leaving the fire chief, he stalked toward them, his gaze on Salem.

Wyatt's arm tightened briefly, then he let go of her. "One of us is in trouble," he said under his breath. "I'm hoping it's you."

John stopped a foot away from her, his hands clamping his hips in the gesture of irritation she was familiar with. "Dammit, Salem. I told you to stay on the boat."

If she hadn't seen the signs of exhaustion in his face, she would have answered him with as much temper as he was displaying. Instead, she lifted her chin and answered simply, "I have a right to be here."

"How do you figure that? Did you take a course in fire fighting at the university?"

"You're here."

John's anger dissipated. Shaking his head in weary exasperation, he stepped close to her and pulled her into his arms. For a moment, he enjoyed the feel of her against him, alive and unharmed.

"What am I going to do with you?" he murmured.

"I thought we'd figured that out a little while ago."

Considering the devastation behind him, he was surprised to find himself smiling. He released her, then took her hand as he shifted his attention to Wyatt. "You okay?"

"No. I'm mad."

Since his own emotions were bent in that direction, John nodded. "There's nothing more we can do about the fire now. Let's go home."

Sandwiched between the two men, Salem walked back to the cottage. John had planned to take her back to Delta's but she didn't want to leave him, even for one night. When they reached the cottage, she would call Delta to tell her they were all right. The older woman had undoubtedly heard the explosions and the sirens, and had possibly even seen the flames. With a twinge of guilt, Salem knew she should have contacted Delta hours ago anyway. If there had been a phone on the boat, she would have called from there. The boat . . . and John.

Her fingers tightened around his as she remembered the sensual joy she had found in his arms. He glanced at her. Apparently the memories were evident in her eyes, for when she looked up at him, he laced his fingers through hers, as though he was thinking the same thing.

When they reached the cottage, they all were too keyed up to sleep, although exhaustion lay heavily on them. Salem made coffee while John washed the reminders of the fire from his face and arms. Wyatt dug through the cupboards until he found the tin of ginger cookies he had snitched from Connie's kitchen.

The small kitchen table boasted only two chairs, so Wyatt suggested they have the coffee in the living room. Salem guessed that John had taken his anger out on the room after she'd walked out earlier, since it was neat and tidy. She sat on the couch, Wyatt in his favorite chair. They had eaten a couple of cookies apiece when John joined them. He sank heavily onto the couch next to her, and she held out the tin to him.

"This might be your last chance before Wyatt gobbles them all up," she said.

He shook his head. "I phoned Delta at the studio to let her know what's been going on. I told her you were with us."

"Thanks. I hope she wasn't too worried." She brushed off a crumb that had fallen on her thigh. "So what are we going to do to stop these Porto brothers from doing any further damage?"

John snaked his good arm around her waist and pulled her back until she was leaning against him. "You aren't going to do anything. Wyatt and I'll take care of them."

She started to protest, but Wyatt cut her off. "Would I be correct in assuming a truce has been hammered out between you two?" he asked, amusement gleaming in his eyes. "Please humor me and say yes."

Since she wasn't sure exactly what their relationship was at this point, Salem didn't say anything.

John simply nodded and changed the subject. "We're not going to wait around for the Portos to do any more damage. In the morning, after I get this cast off, we're going to pay them a little visit. Notify Charlie, Pierre, and Bubba to stay at the dock and to keep their eyes open. The charters can go out as scheduled. I don't think even the Portos are stupid enough to put tourists at risk."

Wyatt leaned forward in his chair, his forearms

resting on his thighs. "I agree with everything you've said except the part about you having the cast removed. I was there in the emergency room when the doctor said you had to have it on for five to six weeks. Your wrist can't possibly be healed so soon."

Before John could answer, Salem said, "He wants a temporary cast put on so he can go diving."

Wyatt stared at John. "Is all this because of today?" Without waiting for an answer, he said, "Dammit, John. There was a problem with the engine, not an attack by pirates. You know as well as I do that occasionally we have engine trouble. It wouldn't have made any difference if you were there or not."

John didn't bother arguing, and Wyatt threw up his hands in defeat. Once John made up his mind about something, that was it. It would be easier to roll a boulder up a cliff than to convince him there might be another way of doing something.

The day's events were catching up with Salem, and she could barely keep her eyes open, but there was something she had been meaning to ask. "Why are the Porto brothers doing all this? Just because of one salvage contract?"

Wyatt chuckled. "This last contract was sort of the last straw. During the past year, we've taken three contracts away from them, but this one must have really hurt. John made a deal with a tourist agency in Miami that handles a lot of package tours. They had been about to sign with Porto Brothers when John undercut them in price."

"There has to be more to it than that." She turned to John. "Have you tried to talk to them?"

Leaning his head against the back of the couch, he said wearily, "Twice. The first time I met with all three of them, Frank, Merlin, and Tom. The second time it was just with Frank, the oldest brother and the major owner of the company."

"And?"

"And nothing. Both times they denied any involvement. Frank made certain veiled references about how easily accidents can happen on boats."

She frowned. "Their reactions are pretty childish. All the charter boats are underbid at one time or another. That's part of the business."

"They evidently don't look at it that way. They're taking it personally." He glanced at her. "I'd like to know why they offered you a job. I checked on their business, and they don't have any contracts that would require a marine biologist. Apparently, they've done their homework on our company and know about your connection to us. But it doesn't make sense that they would want you to work for them. It would be like having the enemy in their camp."

It was the first Wyatt had heard about the Porto Brothers' job offer. As John explained, Salem dropped her head onto his shoulder and closed her eyes. His arm was holding her firmly against his side, and his body was hard and solid and warm. So much had happened that day, she was exhausted and emotionally drained. She would just close her eyes for a few minutes while John talked to Wyatt. She didn't want to think about threats and explosions. She would rather think about the hours spent in John's arms, the only place she ever wanted to be.

* * *

A muffled sound of irritation drew Salem out of a deep sleep. As she began to open her eyes, she heard the sound again and realized it was coming from her. Something was preventing her from rolling over onto her side. Dragging her heavy lids up, she saw what it was. John's arm was resting just under her breasts, one leg thrown over hers.

Scarcely breathing, she looked at the open window, its curtains billowing in the breeze. Her sleep-fogged brain chugged out the information that there shouldn't be a window on that wall in her bedroom. Therefore, she deduced, this wasn't her bedroom.

Turning her head, she saw John asleep beside her, sharing her pillow. His breathing was slow and even, his body relaxed and firm against her side. He had removed his shirt but still wore his jeans. A glance down her own body showed her dressed in what she'd worn the night before.

Even in sleep, John emanated a strength and power she would always associate with him. He had been many things in her life, and now he was her lover. She had no idea what changes that would create in their lives, and whether it would be a temporary situation or a permanent one.

It wasn't the first time she had wakened to find him lying beside her. She remembered one occasion when she was eleven. She'd been ill with the flu, and he had held her when she'd been sick, cooled her brow with damp cloths, and stayed with her all night. Another time she had foolishly gone to a scary movie with Wyatt and had had a nightmare afterward. John had been downstairs at Delta's and had heard her scream. He'd rushed into her room and held her the rest of the night. He'd always been there for her. While Wyatt had been her playmate, John had been the only anchor in her life.

Until she turned sixteen.

Salem raised her hand and gently pushed back the lock of his dark hair that had fallen across his forehead. She hadn't the faintest idea how she had gotten to his bed, but right now she didn't care. She would horde these memories against the time when they were all she had. Her background as an orphan had taught her to cling to the moment, not to pin many hopes on an uncertain future. Her situation was vastly different now, and over the years, she had gained confidence in herself, especially the last four years in Seattle. But she still recognized the insecurity deep within her.

Their early lives in the orphanage had drawn them closer together than many people ever experienced, yet she wondered if she really knew John or just thought she did. He was a man who kept his inner feelings safely locked up within himself. She could only hope she would eventually find the key.

Whether it was the feel of her fingers in his hair or the soft sigh that escaped her, John opened his eyes and looked directly at her, instantly awake.

"Good morning," he said.

She smiled. "Good morning. How did I end up here?"

"You fell asleep while Wyatt and I were talking, and I didn't have the heart to wake you and take you to Delta's. It wasn't much of a hardship to put you in my bed."

She dropped her hand, but John caught it and curled his fingers around it, holding it against his chest. For the first time in weeks, he'd slept through the night. Instead of having to face the long dark hours alone, he'd been able to hold Salem in his arms.

"A man could get used to this," he murmured, "waking up beside you every morning."

She could feel his heartbeat accelerate against her hand. Or was it her own? she wondered vaguely, entranced by the sensual awareness in his eyes.

"Any man," she asked, "or you?"

A corner of his mouth curved upward. "Do you need to have it spelled out?"

She nodded. "Earlier yesterday you were pushing me away. Last night you made love to me. I don't want to take anything for granted."

"I've given you a hard time, haven't I? If it's any consolation, it hasn't been any easier for me."

When she was eighteen, she might have been able to drift along in a fog of contentment, taking each day as it came, so long as she could be with John. Now she needed to know where she stood.

"So where do we go from here?"

John easily recognized the uncertainty in her eyes. The feeling was deeply embedded in his own mind. The only difference was Salem was willing for him to see it. "Now I think we should get to know each other."

She stared at him. "John, I've known you since I was seven years old."

He smoothed his hand over her stomach, his thumb brushing the lower curve of her breast. "That was different. I always made the rules. You came to Key West because that's where I wanted to go. I arranged for you to live at Delta's so you would have some female companionship, instead of being with Wyatt and me all the time. You went to college because I wanted you to go." He cupped her breast, watching her eyes glaze with arousal. "Our relationship has changed now, Salem. You're no longer a child but a woman with rights and opinions of your own. If we stand any chance at all, it has to be on equal terms. Anything less would be cheating both of us."

She was having trouble thinking rationally as she felt him hard against her thigh, his fingers warm and intimate on her breast. Still, she agreed with everything he said. Up to a point. It was what he hadn't said that left an empty place within her. He hadn't said anything about love.

"So you're suggesting we have an affair?"

He leaned over and kissed her briefly. "Honey, we've been having an affair for the last four years. It was just never consummated until last night."

She hadn't thought of it in quite that way before, but he was right. What surprised her more than anything was that he had realized it. But then the statement he'd made in Seattle rose within her, seeping through the sensual response of her body. He'd said she didn't know who she was. He could make love to her, yet even though his background was the same as hers, he wouldn't consider her as someone suitable for a permanent relationship.

John's hand stilled when he saw the shadows in her eyes. "What's wrong, Salem?"

She shook her head. "It doesn't matter."

"I think it does," he said quietly.

Their relationship was so new and so frail. She wasn't sure it could stand up to soul-searching questions yet. Besides, she wasn't confident she would like to hear the answers.

"How do you propose we conduct this affair?" she asked brightly. "Delta wouldn't approve of us living together, and Connie would come after both of us with one of her meat cleavers. They've made their views on living in sin obvious more than once."

And Salem had her own views, John realized as he continued to watch her carefully. "I haven't had time to think much about the details. When I went to find you last night, I was either going to strangle you or give you a thorough tongue-lashing for worrying everyone. Then I touched you, and all I could think of was being inside you. I didn't plan on making love to you, which is one of the other things we have to talk about. I didn't protect you last night. I could use the excuse that I wasn't expecting to make love to you so I didn't come prepared, but to be honest, I didn't think about it until after it was too late."

Salem's lips parted in surprise, her hand sliding down to rest below her waist. She hadn't even thought of the possibility of becoming pregnant, and for a few seconds she wondered if she could be carrying his child. But when she recalled that he had said they were going to have to talk about protection, she removed her hand. He hadn't bluntly said he didn't want her to get pregnant, but since he also hadn't said anything about marriage, she drew her own conclusions.

Still gazing at her, John wondered what she was thinking about that would cause such conflicting emotions to flicker across her face. In the past he'd usually been able to read her expressive eyes, but somewhere during the last four years, she had learned to shield her emotions. He had wanted her to grow up so she would be able to know exactly what she wanted. He hadn't considered there would be a drawback to her maturing. The young girl had worn her emotions on her sleeve. The woman in his arms wasn't nearly as transparent.

They had taken a giant step forward by becoming lovers, but there was still a great deal of territory to cover.

He slid his hand down to rest on the same place hers had been seconds before, thinking about the possibility of their child growing inside her. For so long he'd been preoccupied with the charter business and with Salem. The thought of having a child had been something for the distant future. Until now.

No, he told himself. Contemplating becoming a father had to be shoved aside. It was too soon. They had just become lovers after years of estrangement. They needed time to heal the past before they discussed the future.

To settle the issue of birth control and bring her back from her thoughts, he said, "I'll take care of it."

"All right," she murmured, then slipped out from under his hand, sliding her legs over the side of the mattress. "I don't know what time it is, but I need to get over to Delta's to shower and change clothes. Wyatt will be irritated if I hold him up from going out to the site."

John's hand closed over her arm, tugging her back down beside him. His weight kept her there as he leaned over her.

"Wyatt isn't expecting you at the dock today."

She couldn't hold back the delicious tremors of

reaction at the feel of his hard body on hers. "Why not?" Her voice was oddly breathless.

"I told him you were going to spend the day with me. Do you have a problem with that?"

She shook her head.

He brought his hand up to the side of her face, his thumb stroking her moist bottom lip. "The last four years have been rough on both of us, especially since I saw you in Seattle. I think we deserve to take a day off to be together."

She should complain because he was making plans without consulting her, right after saying they should be on equal terms. Instead, she twined her arms around his neck to bring his head down to hers.

His response was automatic, everything she could have asked for. He kissed her deeply, and she felt a possessiveness in the way he touched her. And desire, as strong and as potent as before, making her heart race. She wrapped her arms around him and gave in to the wondrous sensations soaring through her.

The day they spent together was like a blank page out of a book that they filled with intimate smiles, gentle touches, and white-hot need.

Even the simple procedure of fixing breakfast together became something unique and special. The occasional brush of a hand or a tender look was enough to satisfy them for the moment. They were with each other, at peace finally after being at war for so long. For now that was enough.

John accompanied her to Delta's. While she showered and changed clothes, he went to the kitchen to tell Connie they wouldn't be there for dinner. He didn't explain why, nor did he mention where Salem had spent the previous night. He had the feeling Connie, with her usual perception, had already guessed.

If Connie approved or disapproved of the change in their relationship, she didn't let either show when Salem came back downstairs. She did give her frank opinion of John's getting his cast removed so soon. Using several phrases in her own language, she made it clear she thought it was an incredibly stupid thing to do. Not that it made any difference.

When they were back in the Jeep and headed for the clinic, Salem turned to him, frowning. "How many people have to tell you it's wrong for you to have the cast removed so soon before you'll listen?"

"The cast restricts me too much," he said calmly. He flicked a glance in her direction and noticed her frown. "I'm not being stubborn or having a macho attack. If the circumstances were different, I would be able to take the time for the wrist to heal in the cast. I don't like feeling helpless."

Salem realized with a jolt that she had forgotten about the Porto brothers. That was a good indication of how immersed she'd been in John's company. "What have you and Wyatt decided to do?"

"After I get the cast off this morning, I'm going to try to get a restraining order on them. A little piece of paper won't stop them, but at least they'll know we're on to them."

"Couldn't you press charges after the explosion last night?"

"It was definitely set," he said, turning the

Jeep into the parking lot of the clinic, "but there's no proof the Portos were responsible."

"And if the restraining order doesn't work?"

"We'll try something else."

"I still don't understand why they're doing all this. You've lost contracts without resorting to beating up the crews of the competitor's boats."

He maneuvered the Jeep into a parking space and shut off the engine, then turned to her. "We've heard a few rumors that they're having severe financial problems. They bought several new boats when they thought they were getting the contract with the travel agency. It's possible they could be in danger of losing the boats or even going bankrupt. They have the reputation of being hotheads, slugging first and thinking later. It could be they need someone to blame and we're it, because we got the contract they were depending on."

"Something has to be done before anyone gets hurt again or maybe even killed. Perhaps if I talked to them, I—"

"No," he said strongly. "I don't want you involved in any of this, Salem. Promise me you'll do as I ask and let Wyatt and me take care of it. The Porto brothers already know about your connection with the fleet. If they knew how much you meant to me, they might use you against us somehow, either by threatening you or hurting you in some way. I can't let that happen. I'd rather they blew up every boat we have than have you suffer a scratch."

Salem's heart lurched painfully in her chest. It was the first time he'd given any indication of the depth of his feelings for her. She had known he wanted her physically, but there was a big difference between lust and love. One could exist without the other. Hope began to grow within her like a dormant seed finally getting some vital rain.

She leaned over and kissed him. "Since you asked and didn't order, I'll promise to stay out of it." She didn't add that she would do so only as long as neither Wyatt nor John was hurt in any way. Then she would have to do something, even though she had no idea what it might be.

As he turned to open her door, John brought her back to him. He took her mouth with blatant hunger, his lips parting hers to let him inside. They had been lovers only a short time, too soon for their lovemaking to be taken for granted. His kisses were as potent as before, but she sensed a difference in the way he touched her and kissed her. The desperate quality of his embrace had been replaced by a possessive tenderness that was as intoxicating as the finest wine.

He wasn't a man who made impassioned romantic overtures, but she didn't feel cheated without them. The way he slanted his mouth over hers, caressed her, was a form of communication more intimate and compelling than words could ever equal. A simple look from John could arouse her more deeply than any vow of eternal love from someone else.

All too soon he raised his head and looked down at her, an enticing smile curving his mouth. His expression promised a finish to what the kiss had started.

He held her hand as they walked into the clinic and didn't release her even as a nurse led him into an examining room. Salem stood near a wall, out of the way, while the physician tried to talk John out of having the cast removed. She could have told the doctor he was wasting his breath. He eventually came to the same conclusion and sent in a technician to saw off the cast.

After John's arm had been cleaned off, the doctor returned with an elastic bandage, which he wrapped around the broken wrist. Then he put on a different cast, one made of foam padding and strong plastic, extending from below the elbow to cover part of the hand. John only nodded in acknowledgment when he was warned he would suffer more pain now. As he had before, he turned down the offer of pain medication.

When they returned to the Jeep, she noticed he winced as he used his right hand to turn the key in the ignition. If it had been anyone else, she would have offered to drive, but she knew John well enough to keep silent. While he drove, he kept his arm resting in his lap, using only his left hand on the steering wheel.

After a short visit with their lawyer, who agreed to get a restraining order served on Porto Brothers, John suggested they have lunch somewhere. Because she had seen pain flicker in his eyes every time he moved his arm, she made a different suggestion.

"I'm really not in the mood for crowds right now. I'd rather we pick up some takeaway and go back to the cottage instead."

He nodded in agreement and drove to a restaurant at the marina. A short time later they returned to the Jeep carrying bags containing babyback ribs, salads, and freshly baked bread.

When the wind off the Gulf blew Salem's mauve skirt up, briefly revealing her thigh, a teenager passing by blew a loud wolf whistle in appreciation. John caught her amused smile as she brushed her skirt down.

"I know how he feels," he said as he started the Jeep. "You are the most beautiful woman I've ever seen, Salem."

She heard the rasp of desire in his voice and turned to look at him. Because he said such things rarely, she stored each tender word away like a precious gem. He said even more with his eyes as he met her gaze, mesmerizing her with the sensual fire in their depths. The air around them seemed to crackle with the intensity of the sexual awareness springing up between them.

One advantage of Key West was that it was so small, it didn't take them long to drive to the cottage. Still, by the time they set their food on the kitchen counter, Salem was shaking with a nearly overpowering need. Instead of unpacking the bags, she turned to face John.

He lifted his hand to cup her face, examining each feature slowly. "You make me feel weak and strong at the same time," he murmured. "I want you so badly, I'm surprised I can still stand up. When I'm inside you, I feel as though I could conquer the world. Why do you think that is?"

She shook her head. "I don't know, but I feel the same way. In fact, if you don't put your arm around me soon, I might fall."

He continued to gaze into her eyes as he slid his hand down her back. With his forearm pressed against her bottom, he began to gather up the material of her skirt. She leaned into him when she felt his palm stroke the bare flesh of her thighs. Her lips parted as she sighed his name.

A single finger slipped under the elastic of her panties as he bent his head to cover her open mouth. Her skin was like hot silk, and her taste exploded inside him in a molten heat.

He buried his face against her neck. "You've driven me crazy for a long time, but nothing like this. I don't think I can even make it to the bedroom."

Her hands gripped his shoulders as she sank to the floor, inviting him to come with her.

Seven

Their takeout meal had to be reheated before they finally got to it late in the afternoon. After they had recovered from the tumultuous lovemaking in the kitchen, John had taken her hand and led her to his bedroom. Their need had been so immediate earlier, they had only removed the clothing necessary to come together. Rain began to strike the window as he stripped off her clothes, then his own, and brought her down onto the bed with him. The embers of passion hadn't been fully extinguished, needing only the stroke of a hand to ignite them into flames.

Exhausted eventually, they slept for several hours, desire awakened again as soon as they opened their eyes. Instead of diminishing, their need for each other grew in intensity. They had four years of hunger to satisfy.

By the time they had showered and dressed, the rain was slamming against the cottage. The wind had picked up, turning a gentle summer shower into a gale.

While Salem warmed up their meal, John radioed each boat in the fleet to see if they had made it in before the storm hit. They were all safely tied up at the dock. That should have relieved John, but the skipper of the *Gypsy II* had been oddly evasive when John asked if they had run into any problems, and he signed off before John could ask him any further questions. Other than going down to the dock, John's only option was to wait for Wyatt to return.

"Is everything all right?" Salem asked when he joined her in the kitchen.

"All the boats are in and secured."

That didn't exactly answer her question, but she let it go. Having missed a couple of meals the previous day and lunch that day, she was famished. She might be able to live on love alone, but her stomach was protesting.

They sat down at the small kitchen table, their feast spread out between them. John watched in fascination as she took a bite out of a babyback rib covered generously with barbecue sauce. When she licked sauce off her fingers, he felt his body harden. He shook his head in bemusement.

"Salem, I'm going to need a cast somewhere else than my wrist if you don't stop that."

She ran her tongue over her forefinger. "Stop what?" she asked with mock innocence.

His gaze lowered to her mouth. "That. Wyatt will be walking in the door any minute. The fact that I haven't checked in with the boats until just now will give him enough to smirk about."

She grinned. "You had other things on your mind."

His mouth went dry as she gazed at him with glittering devilment dancing in her eyes. As a child, she had captivated him with her joy for life. She had found pleasure in simple things—a pretty shell, a flower, a beautiful passage in a book. She had lightened the dark corners of his life.

Grown up, Salem could make him her slave.

In the waning light, she looked exotic, like a primitive princess with her mass of dark hair framing her face. Over the years, he had often dreamed of having her naked in his arms. His imagination hadn't even come close to the beauty he had found when he removed the barrier of her clothing.

He was discovering that having her physically wasn't nearly enough to satisfy him. She would still withdraw inside herself at times, making him wonder what she was thinking. He wanted to know all of her—her thoughts, her emotions, her feelings.

But there were other things they needed to discuss at the moment. "As much as I would like you to stay here with me, you know you should go back to Delta's tonight."

Some of the light went out of her face. "Yes. I know."

It was not what she wanted either. It wouldn't bother her to live openly with John, but she knew it would upset Delta considerably. Even though the older woman was eccentric in some ways, Delta had high moral standards. She wouldn't condone Salem's living with a man without benefit of marriage. As much as Salem would like to be with John, she couldn't hurt the woman who had nearly been a mother to her.

John glanced at the rain-streaked window. "I'll come by for you around six in the morning unless this storm keeps up. If we can't go out, I'll come by around eight, and we'll find something to do."

"If the weather keeps the boats in, I should help out in Delta's gallery."

He shrugged and reached for another rib. "I'll go to the gallery with you, then."

"John, you would go crazy standing around in the gallery all day."

"I've gone past crazy, Salem," he drawled, his eyes glowing with sensual warmth. "I understand that you feel obligated to help Delta in the gallery. You have to understand that now that we're lovers, it won't be easy for me to have you out of my sight. When a fantasy comes true, it's impossible to take it for granted."

Salem lowered her gaze to the plate. What about later? she wondered. Would he take their intimacy for granted once the newness had worn away? He still gave no indication he was interested in marriage.

She had known John for over thirteen years. The one subject they had never discussed in all that time was the orphanage. As soon as they had left Boston, they had looked ahead, never back. Yet even as a child, she had sensed John's frustration and anger at having to live under the rules and restrictions of the institution. Once away from that, he had chosen to work for himself for the same reason he'd chosen work that took him out into the open sea. Freedom.

The desire for freedom could be one of the reasons he didn't make any promises to her for the future.

She was roused from her dark thoughts by the front door's slamming shut, then stomping footsteps in the hall. Raising her head, she met

John's amused glance. Wyatt was announcing his arrival with as much subtlety as a Sherman tank.

When he entered the kitchen, Wyatt grinned at the sight of food on the table. "Oh, good. You saved some for me. I'm starving."

While he proceeded to pile the remaining food onto a plate, John asked, "How did it go today?"

Since there was nowhere else to sit, Wyatt hiked himself onto the counter. He didn't answer until he had taken a generous bite out of a succulent rib. "It was unusually quiet," he said at last, his eyes shining with amusement. "The skipper said the radio remained blissfully silent all day. I could have told him you had other things on your mind besides checking up on the fleet, but I didn't."

"I appreciate that," John said. "How much ground did you cover?"

Wyatt made him wait again as he finished off the first rib and picked up another. "I might have found a ballast stone," he said casually.

Both Salem and John stared at Wyatt as he continued to munch on the rib. Since ballast stones were one of the signs of a ship's having sunk, it was a good piece of news. There was no way of knowing whether a ballast stone was from a galleon or a merchant ship until the site was investigated thoroughly. The scholastic foundation that had hired the Gypsy Fleet hadn't insisted on any one sunken vessel, specifying only that they wanted a galleon that would have served as an escort for heavily laden merchant ships. The archaeological specialists were more interested in what they would learn from a working ship than the gold and silver they might find on a merchant ship.

John nodded slowly, too experienced to get overly optimistic. "We'll check it out tomorrow if the weather clears."

"I had just spotted the shape," Wyatt said, "and thought it might be a ballast stone, when the skipper hauled me out of the water because of the approaching storm." He waved the rib in their general direction. "So what have you two been doing today while I slaved away for the good of the Gypsy Fleet?" His sharp gaze fell on the plastic cast on John's wrist. "Other than trade the fiberglass cast for that bit of plastic?"

John pushed back his chair. "We managed to keep busy. I'm going to take Salem home." He caught the younger man's eye, his expression serious. "We need to go over a few things tonight, so hold off going out until I get back."

Wyatt nodded, then glanced at Salem. "See you tomorrow, brat."

She could tell by John's stance, he was impatient to get going. Still she said, "I'll clean off the table first."

John shook his head. "I'll do it when I get back."

Wyatt wiped his hand on a towel, then dug into the pocket of his shorts. "I'm parked behind your Jeep. Take mine."

John automatically raised his right hand to catch the keys, and nearly dropped them as pain shot up his arm. Scowling, he turned and strode out of the kitchen.

Wyatt and Salem exchanged glances. "There's a bit of Missouri mule in that man," Wyatt said softly. "Couldn't you talk him out of getting that cast off?"

"You know him better than that. When has he

ever let anyone talk him out of doing something he wanted to do? I don't have as much influence over John as you seem to think I do." Without giving Wyatt a chance to answer, she brought up the subject she had avoided all day. "How serious do you think this situation is going to get with the Porto brothers? They've attacked John and a couple of crewmen and blown up the boat shed. Something has to be done before someone gets hurt worse, or even killed."

"We're working on it," he answered unsatisfactorily. Glancing toward the doorway, he added, "You'd better scoot. He's waiting for you."

Feeling as though she had just been patted on the head like a child, she scowled at Wyatt and walked out of the room. Maybe there wasn't anything she could do about stopping the Porto brothers, but she didn't like being excluded. Nor was she stupid. The situation could get real ugly if the Portos continued their siege of vandalism and violence toward the Gypsy Fleet. People she cared about were involved. Therefore, she was involved, whether John and Wyatt liked it or not.

The drive to Delta's was short and relatively silent. John walked her to the side porch, but didn't come in. They stood under the protection of a small roof, the rain and wind forgotten completely as they stared at each other. After a moment, he kissed her swiftly, touching only her mouth.

When he raised his head, he looked down at her, yet was unable to see her eyes clearly in the darkness. "I hate this," he said hoarsely. "You belong with me in my bed, not here."

His words conjured up memories of the hours spent in his arms, and she ached to have his arms around her again, to feel him deep inside her, part of her.

Shoving her hands into her skirt pockets to keep them from reaching out to him, she couldn't hold back the shiver that ran through her. And it wasn't from the rain or cool air. "We agreed," she said. "This is how it has to be under the circumstances."

He sighed heavily. "I don't have to like it."

She wanted to scream at him that there was something he could do about it, but she didn't. Instead, she turned to the door. "I'll see you tomorrow."

She was gone before he could stop her. John stood rooted to the porch, until a gust of wind blew cold rain over him. Cursing under his breath, he ran to the Jeep. Sitting behind the wheel, he forgot about the storm outside. A more severe one was roaring inside him. The night before, when he had held Salem while she slept, he had decided to give her the courtship she deserved. He didn't regret making love to her without the usual preliminaries of dating. She had given herself freely to him with all the passion he could ever hope for, and he'd seen no signs of regret.

He had done so many things wrong with her in the past, wasted so much time, that he wanted to make it up to her by giving her a little of the romance she deserved. Hell, he admitted, it was what he wanted for himself. His life might have been unconventional from the start, but that didn't mean he couldn't abide by a few traditions now.

Somehow, he would take his time with her, court her properly. Then, when he felt the time

was right, he would ask her to marry him. He
would let Wyatt have the cottage and find a house
where they could raise a family and live happily
ever after. All he had to do was to be patient.
Knowing Salem would be his wife eventually
would make up for all the lonely nights he was
going to have to endure without her.

He swore again, this time aloud, when he
turned the key and pain stabbed his wrist. From
experience, he knew wishing things were different didn't make them so. It was up to him to
change them.

Salem's scent lingered in the close confines of
the Jeep, and the slightest whiff of it tightened
his body. He clenched his jaw. This might be one
of the shortest courtships on record.

During the next four days, Salem became
increasingly confused. Each morning John arrived
at Delta's to take her to the dock. He stayed
aboard the boat while she and Wyatt explored the
seabed for signs of the wreckage. The object Wyatt
had thought was a ballast stone turned out to be
a long rectangular strip of dead coral. They were
disappointed but not surprised. Each evening,
John drove her back to Delta's, dropping her off
so she could shower and change for dinner. The
first night they went out to eat, but dined with
Delta and her guests the other two nights. At a
reasonable hour, John would leave, kissing her
briefly when she walked him to the door. On the
fourth day the last of the guests departed, and no
others arrived to take their place. Salem wondered if that was Delta's choice or just a
coincidence.

There had been no further incidents of violence. At least none that she was aware of. Since she was with Wyatt and John all day and with John in the evening, she thought she would have known if something else had happened.

On the fourth night, Friday night, she was too restless to sleep. John's attitude toward her, the short unsatisfying good-night kisses and his casual "I'll see you in the morning" totally baffled her. Refusing to spend another night staring at the ceiling, she put on her robe and went out to Delta's studio. One advantage of Delta's nocturnal working hours was that she was always available for midnight conferences.

Delta's studio was about the size of a two-car garage and set apart from the main house, not so much by distance as by a profusion of high shrubs. The pleasant odor of paint and varnish permeated the air, a scent as familiar as the fragrance of Connie's rose garden. Wearing a denim smock, with several slender brushes stuck behind one ear, Delta stood in front of the rosewood easel in the center of the room under an array of lights. Unlike many other artists, Delta didn't believe that a painter could work only under the clear northern light. Her creative juices flowed at night, and she was content with artificial lighting.

Shelves filled one wall of the studio, and Delta had crammed a wide array of supplies on them without regard to neatness or category. Opposite the shelves was a sofa laden with fluffy pillows. A low table sat in front of it, and several comfortable chairs faced the sofa. A floor lamp was tucked behind the sofa at one end.

Although cluttered and seemingly disorganized, the studio was clean and inviting.

"I was wondering," Delta said without turning around, "when you would be trotting down here to talk."

Salem sank into the lumpy sofa that was older than she. "Have I been that obvious?"

"Not to the others perhaps."

"Well, that's something, I suppose," Salem said ruefully.

Delta added one more stroke of paint to the canvas, then put down her brush. Pulling a rag from a pocket in her smock, she wiped her hands as she walked over to a rattan chair near the sofa.

She sighed with relief after sitting down. "I find standing for long hours isn't as easy as it used to be. It must be true what the calendar indicates. I'm getting older."

Salem shook her head. "Not you, Delta. You will never get old."

Delta smiled. "It's sweet of you to think so, dear, but bones sometimes age faster than the spirit." She tilted her head to one side, studying Salem with her sharp eyes. "That's one thing I've always admired about you, your spirit. Although I must say it's been slightly diminished the last couple of days. I remember a young girl who faced each day with her chin held high and a sparkle in her eyes. She was never afraid to tackle something, whether it was difficult or not. Which, I might add, has been partly responsible for some of the gray hair I've acquired over the years. There were times I wished you were a trifle more cautious in some of your endeavors, like when you climbed the banyan tree just because Wyatt dared you. You were always the most determined little girl and young woman I've ever seen, and that makes me wonder why you've been so quiet lately."

"I'm in love with John."

Delta nodded. "And?"

Salem's mouth twisted in a grimace. "You don't seem at all surprised. Have I been obvious about that too?"

"Yes," the artist replied bluntly. "Now why is being in love with John Canada a problem?"

"A few days after I came back last week, we became closer than we'd been in the past. He finally sees me as a woman and not a little girl. Then, the last four days, he has been so solicitous and polite, I don't even know him. All of a sudden, he's taking me out to dinner, pulling out my chair, opening doors for me." She threw her hands up. "Yesterday he brought me a rose he'd picked from Connie's garden, for Pete's sake. He's like a stranger." Delta's smile broadened until she was grinning like the Cheshire cat. "What's so darn funny?" Salem asked indignantly.

Delta laughed until tears ran down her cheeks. Finally, when she was able to catch her breath, she explained. "Apparently, I've left a few important facts out of your upbringing, darling. The man is wooing you."

Salem couldn't have been more surprised if Delta had announced she was going to run off with the mailman. Sounding like an asthmatic train, she sputtered, "He's woo-woo what?"

"Wooing you. Courting you. Whatever it's called nowadays when a man wants to cultivate a relationship with a woman. Really, Salem, to complain about a man pulling out a chair for you and bringing you flowers is unbelievable."

All Salem could do for a few seconds was stare

at Delta as her words sank in. "Why would he feel he needed to do all that now?" she blurted out without thinking.

Delta pursed her lips. "After you've become lovers, you mean?"

Salem shook her head, in awe of the older woman's perception. "Nothing gets past you, does it? You see us for only several hours every evening, yet you know everything that's going on."

"One of the requirements for an artist is to be observant. I've also known both of you a long time."

Salem met Delta's frankness with her own. "Are you disappointed?"

"Forgive the unflattering analogy, but you and John were like a pot simmering on a back burner for ages. You were bound to boil over eventually. To answer your question, I'm not disappointed you have slept together before marriage. Love is rare and should be celebrated. But I am pleased John is trying to do things in the correct manner now."

"I'm not sure I agree with you that he's courting me. We don't need to go through the ritual of dating to get to know each other. We've known each other for years. He should know I don't need romantic gestures."

"Maybe he needs to make them."

Salem digested the simple statement for a long moment. It was a perspective she hadn't considered. "Maybe he does." She reached into the pocket of her skirt. "There's another problem."

Delta leaned forward to take the envelope Salem handed to her. "What's this?"

"I've been offered a position with a corporation in Monterey, California, that has established a

marine center on Monterey Bay. They do oceano-
graphic research, along with displaying various
aspects of sea life to the public for purposes of
education. They sent me the paperwork they need
before I start work in September."

After briefly scanning the papers, Delta folded
them and inserted them back into the envelope.
"You haven't filled these out. Does that mean you
aren't going to take the position?"

"I don't know. It depends."

"On John?"

Salem couldn't help smiling at the frank question. Delta had always shot from the hip, and her
advice and opinions were usually right on target.
"He knows I've had the job offer. When he came
to Seattle for my graduation, he said I should do
well there. He hasn't mentioned it again."

Delta chuckled. "He's obviously had other things
on his mind lately. Give him time, child. I realize
patience has never been one of your strong
points, but in this case, I suggest you use every
ounce you have. He'll get around to discussing
the future when the present settles down."

Salem wished she were as confident as Delta.
She reached for the envelope and returned it to
her pocket. "I'll wait a little longer before I send
the papers back."

Adjusting a brush that was slowly slipping forward over her ear, Delta smiled. "I think that's
wise."

They both turned to look when they heard the
door opening. Connie entered, carrying a tray
with a teapot, three cups, and a plate of cookies.
Salem didn't even ask why Connie had brought
three cups instead of two. Somehow the housekeeper always knew where everyone was without

being told. Her full red skirt flowed around her legs as she walked gracefully across the studio to place the tray on the table in front of the sofa.

Not wanting to intrude on the nightly tea ceremony between Delta and Connie, even though Connie had intended to include her, Salem started to get up. "I'll see you both in the morning."

Connie poured tea into three cups. "Sit down and have some tea, child. John is on his way here. I told him we would be in the studio."

"John is coming here? At this hour?" she asked in surprise. "Why?"

"I phoned him."

Delta got to the heart of the matter. "What's happened?"

"A man came to the front door, asking to see Salem. He was not someone I knew or cared to know. Nor would he be someone Salem would know. He was not pleasant when I told him Salem was not in the house." She smiled at Salem. "I told him the truth. You were not in the house."

"What did he look like?"

Connie described him in detail—six feet tall, sun-bleached blond hair, the tattoo of an eagle on his forearm, needed a shave, and a rough manner. Salem had no idea who the man was, although she had an idea who might have sent him. "Did he say why he wanted to see me?"

"No," Connie said. "But he did not leave entirely. He is sitting in a truck parked across the street, watching the house. That is why I phoned John. He will—"

She stopped as they faintly heard an engine being revved up, then the harsh noise of screeching tires. Connie calmly walked back to the door, standing to one side so she would be behind the door when it was opened. Salem turned off the floor lamp beside the sofa. The lights over the easel still illuminated the room, but she and Delta were in shadow.

They heard the sound of running footsteps, growing louder as they neared the studio. Then the door burst open, and Wyatt stood in the doorway.

Salem turned the lamp back on while Delta said quietly, "It's Wyatt, Connie."

Connie moved from behind the door and gestured for Wyatt to be seated as though nothing were unusual. "Would you care for some tea?"

"No, thank you, Connie," he said tightly.

Salem stared at the empty doorway behind Wyatt, and her heart thudded heavily. "Where's John?"

"The guy out front took off as soon as he saw us coming down the street." He included everyone, but his gaze was on Salem. "Is everyone all right?"

"We are fine, Wyatt," Delta said. "Please sit down."

Wyatt pulled up a wooden chair and straddled it, resting his arms across the back. "Take it easy, Salem," he said, noticing her pale face. "John's only going to tail him."

"Why didn't you go with him? They've already beaten him up once."

"So you think it's my turn now?" he asked with amusement. "He told me to come here to make sure you women were safe." He lifted his head as a car door slammed. "That's probably him now."

In case it wasn't John, Wyatt took Connie's previous position behind the door. The three women watched the door open, then relaxed when John stepped inside.

Wyatt looked inquiringly at him, and John shook his head. "I got his license number, but I don't think we really need it to know who sent him."

Making an effort to control his anger, John strode over to the three women, his left hand curled into a fist. "Tell me again what he said when he came to the door, Connie. Are you sure he asked for Salem?"

"Yes. Although I wouldn't say he *asked*. He said he wanted to see Salem Shepherd." Then she repeated what she had told Delta and Salem.

John looked at Salem. "Dammit," he said forcefully. "I wish you weren't here."

Eight

Even though she knew John's outburst was due to his worry about her, Salem couldn't stop the pain his words caused her. Lifting her chin defensively, she took a page out of Delta's book on frank speaking. "I think we can assume that if the man was from Porto Brothers, he wasn't interested in trying to hire me as a marine biologist. The only way we'll find out exactly what he wanted is for me to talk to him."

"No!"

Startled by his loud voice, Salem blinked but held her ground. "Why not? You've tried to talk to them, and it didn't work. Maybe if—"

"No," he repeated with less volume but no less authority. "After I talked to them, they sent some goons to the docks to break a few bones. You stay away from them, Salem. If they think nothing of beating people up and blowing up buildings, they wouldn't hesitate to use you to get what they want from us."

John shuddered as he thought of how they

could use her. He'd meant what he had said earlier. He wished to heaven she were anywhere but
Key West. At least until this mess with the Porto
brothers was over. Even though she had tried to
hide it, he'd seen the hurt in her eyes and had
realized she'd misunderstood him. He ground his
teeth in frustration. Once the problem with the
Porto brothers was settled, he was going to take
her somewhere where they would be alone, even
if it was on a boat in the middle of the Gulf.

"John," Delta said quietly, "please sit down so
we can discuss this rationally. I have never seen a
problem yet that can't be solved by clear, concise
brainstorming. Let's all put our heads together on
this one and figure out where we go from here."

Salem wasn't at all surprised Delta considered
their problem her problem. It was the same attitude the older woman had taken fourteen years
earlier when she had brought them all into her
house. As a child, Salem had simply accepted Delta's generosity and warmth of spirit. Now that
she was older and had seen more of life, Salem
understood how exceptional both Delta and Connie were.

While John walked across the studio to get a
chair from the corner, Connie handed the plate
of cookies to Wyatt. Once John was seated, Delta
made a steeple with her fingers, her expression
thoughtful. "It appears that these ruffians aren't
giving up. It might help if we knew why they are
so against the Gypsy Fleet."

"The only thing we can come up with," Wyatt
said, "is that we got a contract they thought they
were going to get."

The older woman shook her head. "There has
to be more than that. These are grown men, not

children throwing a tantrum because they can't have something they want. Surely they've been in that type of situation before. So far, the fleet has been on the receiving end with little recourse other than meeting force with force, which I disapprove of on principle. According to John, there is nothing the authorities can do without any evidence. I suggest we provide them with the proof they need."

"How would we go about doing that?" John asked warily.

Delta glanced at Salem, but before she could say what she was thinking, John shook his head. This time he said the word in a cold, hard voice. "No."

"Let's hear Delta's idea before we turn it down," Wyatt suggested. "Nothing we've done so far has accomplished anything. We can at least listen to what she has to say."

Delta didn't look at John, but continued to watch Salem. "As you all know, this is a very small island where news travels quickly. Apparently our opponents have found out about Salem's relationship with John and Wyatt. The appearance of the Neanderthal at the door this evening would be an indication they have switched their attention from the boats and John and Wyatt to what they might feel is the weakest link. I suggest we let them talk to Salem. It's possible she can find out exactly what their complaint is. It would give us something to work from."

Before John could protest again, Salem asked, "What did you have in mind, Delta?"

"This would require courage and a smattering of bravado, but I think if we all work together, it might work. I have no guests at the moment.

Apparently the Porto brothers are having the house watched and are aware of that fact, considering we had an uninvited visitor here tonight. If Salem sent a message to the Portos that she wishes to speak to them personally rather than to one of their henchmen, she might be able to meet with them."

John shook his head. "They aren't just going to come in and sit down and have a cup of tea, Delta. They don't want to compromise on anything. They want to blow us out of the water for good. It's foolish to put Salem in danger by inviting them into the house with her here alone."

Delta tapped her fingertips together. "Ah, but she wouldn't be alone. We would all make a point of leaving the house. After dinner, you and Wyatt would be seen driving away. Connie could make it look like she was going to visit one of her friends. I, of course, would come here to the studio." Looking exceedingly pleased with herself, she finished by adding, "You and Wyatt can hop over the back fence and enter the house from the back door. Connie could position herself across the street, ready to notify the authorities if they manage to take Salem out of the house before you boys arrive. If necessary, Connie could follow them to see where they've taken her."

Delta looked around at the others. Wyatt was frowning, John was scowling, and Salem was obviously thinking it over.

John gave his opinion first. "I don't like it. After the other things they've done, I can't see them sitting down calmly to discuss the matter with Salem. They're more apt to hold her as a hostage until we sign over the contract or whatever it is they want."

"That's one of the problems we have," Salem said. "We don't know exactly why they're doing all these things. You tried to talk to them, John. It didn't do any good. We're not even sure it's the contract with the travel agency that started this whole thing. It could be something we aren't even aware of. Maybe I could find out what it is. Then we would have something to work with."

Everyone nodded in agreement. Except John. "There has to be some other way. Either Wyatt or I can try to talk to them again. I want Salem out of it."

Salem opened her mouth to protest, but Delta spoke first. "Salem has as much at stake here as you and Wyatt. The fleet means a great deal to her, as do the two of you. If she is willing to do what she can to end this intimidation before it gets any more out of hand, then I believe that should be her choice to make."

His chair scraped on the floor as John got to his feet. It took him only two steps to reach Salem. He took her hand and yanked her off the couch.

"Excuse us," he muttered as he led her to the door. "I want to talk to Salem for a minute."

Once they left the studio, it took a moment for Salem's eyes to adjust to the darkness. John didn't appear to have any difficulty, and he walked quickly around the corner of the house. He stopped under a tall flowing banyan tree but didn't release her hand. His grip was so tight, she was beginning to lose the feeling in the tips of her fingers, but she didn't try to pull her hand away.

The branches of the trees blocked out some of the pale glow from the full moon overhead yet allowed enough illumination for her to see his expression. It wasn't just the shadowy moonlight that made his skin look pale despite his tan. She'd noticed the ashen color when he entered Delta's studio. His eyes were dark and strangely haunted.

"Salem, I don't want you to meet with the Portos. They've shown they aren't just making threats. They're carrying them out. We'll find some other way to stop them."

Since she was eight years old, he had tried to protect her from the various lumps and bumps of growing up. He was still doing it.

She had to make him see she was an adult in every way, not just in his bed. She wanted to be able to lean on him at times, but she also wanted him to feel he could lean on her.

"If there is a chance," she said patiently, without any emotion in her voice, "even a small chance, that I can help, I want to try. I realize I'm not one of the legal owners of the fleet, but it's been a big part of my life too." Her voice changed, hardening with anger. "They broke your wrist, John. They hurt you. Don't you know I would do anything to prevent that from happening again?"

Some of his tension eased as he gazed down at her. The last thing he expected to do was smile, but he couldn't help it.

"What do you plan to do, wildcat?" he asked, stroking her hair. "Whip them single-handedly? I tried, remember? And I'm a lot bigger than you are."

It seemed like it had been forever since he'd touched her. She had to force herself to remember the serious issue they were discussing. "Don't make fun of me, John."

"I'm not making fun of you, honey. If you're half as protective about me as I am about you, I can understand how you're feeling."

"We can't have this threat hanging over us forever. If meeting with them might be a step toward getting this stupid thing resolved, then I want to do it."

For a moment, he didn't say anything. His fingers continued to slide through her hair as he stared into her eyes. "If anything happens to you," he said softly, "I'll go out of my mind."

His statement rocked her, warmed her like the rays of the tropical sun. Because he exposed his emotions so rarely, she reveled in his admission.

She rested her hands against his chest, loving the feel of his strong heartbeat. "Nothing will happen to me. It can't. Fate couldn't be that cruel."

"You don't have to fight my battles for me."

He was astonishingly old-fashioned in some ways, and she found that both endearing and frustrating. "I don't want to fight your battles for you. I want to fight them with you. Kiss me instead of scolding me, John. I've missed you."

He knew what she meant. They had seen each other every day, but usually in the company of others. Lowering his head, he kissed her as his arms brought her pliant body into his. He felt her grab his shirt as he deepened the assault on her mouth, her response as heated as the blood surging through his veins.

The rough edge of fear for her safety collided with sharp need as he savored her taste, her scent, the feel of her breasts crushed against his chest. Without raising his mouth from hers, he turned them until she was leaning against the stout trunk of the tree. Parting his legs, he brought her lower body into the cradle of his hips, nearly exploding with the desire that whipped through him.

With his good hand, he pressed against the back of her thigh until she lifted her knee around his hip, bringing them closer. He groaned as she arched against his aroused loins. Breaking away from her mouth, he brushed his lips over her throat. She tilted her head back, a soft aching sound coming from deep within her.

The sound vibrated through him, drowning out reason. Time and place didn't matter. He had to have her now, feel her heat surround him. As he reclaimed her mouth, he lifted her skirt, and she helped him peel away the only other barrier between him and her naked flesh. With his encasted arm behind her to keep her locked to him, he unsnapped his jeans and shoved them out of the way.

He raised his head to look at her as he cupped her bottom and lifted her against him. The way her eyes changed as he slowly entered her was almost as exciting as feeling her moist heat close around him. Her fingers dug into his shoulders, and she shuddered under the onslaught of uncontrollable sensations as he began to move inside her.

He watched in fascination as her eyes closed in ecstasy, then opened again to meet his gaze. She was the most beautiful, sensual creature in the world, he thought. Then she clasped him deep inside her, and he couldn't think at all.

As though from a long distance, he heard her sigh softly as she collapsed against him, her breathing as labored as his. Disregarding the pain in his wrist, he held her securely as they recovered the intense pleasure they had shared.

She was still leaning against him when he lowered his arms, the pain in his wrist forcing him to release her. With a heavy sigh, she backed away from him to adjust her clothing. Her face was in shadow, and he couldn't see her expression.

If things were different, he thought, they could be lying together in his bed instead of preparing themselves to face the others. After fastening his jeans, he leaned back against the tree.

"We can't keep going on like this, Salem."

Salem heard the quiet intensity in his voice. There was something he could do about it, but obviously marriage hadn't occurred to him. He also hadn't said he loved her.

The black shadow in the back of her mind rushed forward, though she tried to suppress it. Perhaps making their relationship permanent wasn't what he wanted. It irritated her that she could be so sure of his desire but not his love.

She replied as honestly as she could. "I don't like this any better than you do. For now, this is the way it has to be."

John frowned. He had never heard that particular note in her voice before. Defeated. Vulnerable. Pushing himself away from the tree, he cupped his hand under her chin. She looked away, and he forced her to turn until he could see her face. She kept her lashes lowered, hiding her expressive eyes.

"Salem, look at me," he said softly.

A full minute went by before she did as he asked. Her expression was defiant, and he'd seen that look in her eyes when Wyatt used to challenge her to do something he said she couldn't do. Tenderness welled up inside him.

"This isn't the way I had it planned. I wanted to give you a little romance. Instead, there are men blowing up boat sheds and harassing us."

"I don't need to be courted, John," she said quietly. She needed him to say he loved her, to promise her they would be together always.

"It's what I wanted for you." When he paused, they both heard the door to the studio close, then Connie and Wyatt calling good-night to Delta. John took her arm and started to lead her to the house. "Tomorrow some members of the foundation that hired us to find a galleon will be arriving to check our progress. They're going to be here a couple of days. We'll take all the precautions we can for the fleet while they're here. Then after they leave, we'll confront the Portos. All of us. In the meantime, I want you to stay here with Connie and Delta." He felt her stiffen against him. "Dammit, Salem. I need to know you're going to be safe. If necessary, I'll let Wyatt handle the foundation and stay with you to make sure you don't do anything stupid."

He was treating her like a child again, she thought with frustration. She'd assumed they had come a long way when the only thing that had changed was that they'd become lovers.

They rounded the corner of the house and saw Wyatt standing beside the Jeep, waiting for John. As they neared the back steps, Salem stopped and looked up at John. "I won't do anything stupid. Since you don't need me on the boat tomorrow, I'll work in Delta's gallery, then come right back here." Without giving him a chance to debate the issue any further, she waved to Wyatt and walked away from John into the house.

John stared at the closed door, his mind going over every word they had spoken. Why did he feel something was wrong? He knew she didn't like being excluded from things, but he couldn't help it. The situation with the Porto brothers wasn't like some of the problems they'd had when they were first starting out with the fleet. She had always worked just as hard as he and Wyatt then, earning her own way without complaint. He could understand why she wanted to help them, but this was different.

He would gladly lose everything he had as long as he didn't lose her.

The next morning, Salem entered the kitchen to find that Delta hadn't gone to bed as she usually did. While Salem fixed her coffee, she explained to Delta about the foundation members arriving to check on the progress of the search for a galleon.

"Since I'm not needed on the boat today," she went on, "I thought I would go to the gallery. Do you suppose Josslyn could use an extra hand?"

"I'm sure she would love to have you in the gallery, but wouldn't it be better if you stayed here today?"

Salem shook her head. "At least I would be doing something useful, even if all I do is dust off the frames."

Stirring a spoonful of honey into the tea Connie had set down in front of her, Delta asked, "Did John talk you out of meeting with the Portos?"

"He said we'll all meet with them after the foundation people leave."

"Maybe that's a better idea than the one I had." Relief was obvious in Delta's voice. "It's difficult to try to be reasonable with unreasonable people. Let's just hope they don't try anything else until you all can sit down and hash out whatever is causing these men to terrorize the fleet."

Salem spent a few more minutes in the kitchen with the two women, although she refused Connie's offer of a big breakfast. In her bedroom she changed into a sage-green skirt and sheer white cotton blouse, then walked the six blocks to the gallery.

Josslyn Hunter had been the manager of Delta's gallery for years. As usual, she was pleased to see Salem and took advantage of the extra pair of hands by asking Salem to mind the showroom while she did the books in the small office in the back. Enough people came in to browse and buy to keep Salem occupied all morning. Over the years Josslyn had taken on other artists' work on consignment, along with an assortment of tasteful crafts that sold well to tourists who were interested in more than seashells and postcards. The one thing that hadn't changed was the way the artwork was cataloged, making it easy for Salem to find the prices and ring up the sales without having to ask Josslyn for help.

Around noon the gallery was empty except for one woman who had been there for about an hour. Josslyn took advantage of the lull to leave the gallery in Salem's hands while she went out to lunch instead of gulping down a sandwich between customers.

Salem was straightening the stack of catalogs

on a small table near the front door when she suddenly felt uneasy. Looking up, she was startled to see the lone woman in the gallery staring at her instead of the painting in front of her. The other woman was in her early twenties, dressed in white linen slacks and a bright pink tunic belted around her slim waist. Her reddish shoulder-length hair was tightly curled and crimped.

But it was the woman's green eyes that held Salem's attention. She was looking at Salem with pure hatred.

"Could I help you find something?" Salem asked.

The woman's sandals sounded unusually loud on the polished wood floor as she slowly walked toward the table. "Are you Salem Shepherd?"

"Yes," she answered cautiously, wondering what the woman's problem was. "Why do you ask?"

"They said you were very beautiful. I just wanted to see you for myself."

Since it didn't sound like a compliment, Salem didn't take it as one. "Well, now you've seen me."

The woman's malevolent gaze flowed over her. "I disagree with them. You aren't as pretty as I am."

Salem had no idea who "they" were, nor did she care. "Look, if you want to look at the paintings in the gallery, feel free, but I'm not one of the local sights. I'll take your money if you want to purchase a painting, but I don't have to take your rudeness."

The other woman raised her hand as though to strike Salem. Standing her ground, Salem stared back at the woman, ready to defend herself if necessary.

Only a few seconds passed before the strange

woman lowered her hand, but it seemed much longer to Salem. She'd never had such overt hatred aimed at her, and it unnerved her, especially when she had no idea what caused it.

The woman's lips tightened into a thin line. "I don't know what he sees in you, but it doesn't matter. I'll make him forget you."

She yanked the front door open, then twisted to look back at Salem. The front of her shirt gaped open. A gold medallion dangled from one of the chains she wore around her neck.

Stunned, Salem watched the woman leave the gallery. What was that all about? she wondered. As far as she knew, she'd never met the woman before. Mulling over what the woman had said, Salem wasn't any wiser than she'd been before. The woman had known her name, so it wasn't a case of mistaken identity.

And she was wearing a medallion, similar in shape to the two-escudo piece Salem wore.

It was the woman's last remark that stuck in Salem's mind. Could the woman mean John? she wondered, hating the thought but unable to come up with any other explanation. The threat didn't matter. Knowing John had been involved with that woman did. At least she didn't need to torture herself with wondering if John was still seeing the woman.

When Josslyn returned, Salem asked her if she'd noticed the woman who had been in the gallery before Josslyn had gone to lunch. Unfortunately, the older woman hadn't. Pretending it didn't matter, Salem smiled and went to help a couple who had picked up one of the wood carvings.

Wyatt was waiting for Salem outside the gallery

when she left at five. She frowned when she saw him, immediately wondering if something was wrong. The fact that he was wearing navy slacks, a white shirt, a tie, and a sport jacket was almost as startling. Since he was smiling at her, she let the coil of tension ease inside her.

Leaving Josslyn to lock up the gallery, Salem walked over to Wyatt, who was leaning nonchalantly against the fender of the Jeep. "It looks like you have a hot date tonight."

Grinning, he opened the passenger door for her. "I'm just the lowly chauffeur, here to escort you to the ball."

Waving good-night to Josslyn, she slid onto the seat. When Wyatt joined her, she asked, "What ball?"

"We're taking the bigwigs from Miami out to dinner. John asked me to bring you. He'd have come for you himself, but he couldn't get away from them. Do you want to change first or powder your nose or whatever you girls do to get ready?"

She laughed. "I'd like to change first. Where are we meeting them?"

Wyatt named one of the better restaurants on the island.

"I definitely need to change."

While Wyatt was checking the rearview mirror before pulling into the traffic, Salem glanced down the street and saw the woman who had been in the gallery earlier.

"Wyatt, who is that woman in front of Kramer's?"

He turned his head to look, but there was no one there. "I don't see anyone."

Salem craned her neck to look back, then up the street. He was right. There was no sign of her anywhere. "That's strange. She was there just a minute ago."

"Why do you want to know who she is?"

"She came into the gallery earlier today." Even though she still felt the uncomfortable chill the other woman's words had caused, she wasn't going to grill Wyatt about John's past involvement with other women. "It doesn't matter."

Wyatt waited for her in the kitchen while Salem dashed up to her room to shower and change. She chose a jade-colored dress that had narrow straps, a curved neckline, and gold buttons down the front. After brushing her hair, she added gold-hoop earrings, but that was the only jewelry she wore other than the gold medallion.

Looking at her reflection in the mirror above the dresser, she touched the medallion, frowning as she thought of the medallion the angry woman wore. The woman had been too far away for Salem to see it clearly, but it had looked remarkably like her own.

Shaking her head to dismiss the thoughts that crept in against her will, she let go of the medallion and grabbed her shawl. She wasn't going to borrow trouble by jumping to conclusions. It wasn't John's past that should concern her. She had enough to think about with the present.

When they entered the restaurant, Wyatt escorted her to a large table toward the back. It was positioned near a wall of glass that offered, a clear, unobstructed view of the sea. Seated at the table with John were three men and one woman. The men were in their fifties, bespectacled, with pale skin and stiff spines. The woman was perhaps in her early forties, trim and fashionably dressed in a becoming gray suit and a crisp white blouse.

As Salem and Wyatt approached the table, the woman was leaning toward John, holding a cigarette to her mouth in a silent invitation for him to light it. He took a matchbook off the table, struck a match, and held it politely as the woman drew on the cigarette. Then he looked up and saw Salem. For a moment, he simply gazed at her, absorbing her. Then he drew the lighted match to his lips and blew out the flame, a corner of his mouth curving slightly.

Pushing back his chair, he stood as Wyatt delivered her to his side as though she were a precious long-awaited package. John made the introductions, alluding to Salem's assistance with the project before seating her in the chair next to him.

Professor Ingleside leaned forward to speak to Salem. "Ah, yes. The marine biologist. We were pleased to hear you were on the team, Miss Shepherd. In fact we might have a use for your expertise in the future. Would you be interested?"

John answered for her. "Salem has other plans. She's going to work for a marine museum in Monterey, California."

The professor made a sound of disappointment. "That's too bad. Keep us in mind if you change your mind. We have a number of scientific projects coming up that are very interesting."

He proceeded to tell them about some of them, but Salem wasn't listening. She was replaying what John had said. She couldn't believe it. He still expected her to leave. What was worse, he didn't sound as though he minded.

She sat numbly beside him, trying to appear as

though nothing were wrong. Luckily, the professors were talkative and filled all the conversational gaps.

The representatives from the foundation were obviously satisfied with the progress, unlike other clients John and Wyatt had worked with who expected immediate results. These were intelligent, experienced people who were willing to bide their time, knowing the results would be worth it. They were greedy for information, not gold.

Salem enjoyed the various stories they told of other projects, some successful, some not, but she was glad when the meal was finally over and coffee was served. Soon after, Wyatt offered to escort them to their hotel, leaving John and Salem alone at the table.

John loosened his tie and undid the collar button. Leaning back in his chair, he sighed deeply. "I know these business dinners are necessary, but they never get any easier."

She smiled faintly. Only someone who knew him well could have seen the impatience in his eyes during dinner. He was a man more comfortable on the deck of a boat than in a boardroom, but he would always do whatever was necessary, even if he hated it.

"They seemed to enjoy themselves, even if you didn't," she said. "In fact, they appeared to be pleased with everything we're doing."

He pushed back his chair and reached for her hand. "No more talk of business tonight. Come dance with me. I need to feel you next to me."

The low huskiness in his voice sent her heart soaring, even as a confusion of thoughts filled her head. She wanted to ask him about the red-haired woman who wore a medallion and hated her guts. She wanted to demand to know where their relationship was going. She felt as though she'd been given a gift, but wasn't sure if she was going to be allowed to keep it.

She tightened her fingers around his hand and followed him to the small dance floor. His arms encircled her, holding her firmly against him. Her breasts were crushed into his chest, and she could feel him exhale sharply, then let out his breath slowly. As she began to move with him, she became aware of the hard ridge of his arousal pressing against her. Having him so close when she was unable to touch him the way she wanted was a refined torture.

John buried his face in her neck, his body shuddering with the need to be inside her. How had he waited so long before making love with her? he wondered. And how much longer could he wait before he was sure of her?

Nine

Whatever plans John had made for the end of the evening, he was forced to change them when he saw Wyatt's Jeep parked in the lot next to the restaurant. Wyatt was not in the Jeep or anywhere near it. The driver's door was ajar.

Salem had to quicken her pace to keep up with John's long strides as he walked over to the abandoned Jeep. "Maybe he went with the people from the foundation for a nightcap," she suggested, knowing John was thinking the worst. After the incidents of the last week, she couldn't really blame him.

"You heard them. They were tired. Besides, Wyatt would have put them off even if they had offered. He had a late date with a woman he's been seeing." He slammed his fist down on the fender of the Jeep. "Damn them. If they do anything to him, I'll see they rot in hell."

Salem knew whom he was referring to and was very much afraid he was right. In an attempt to diffuse his anger before he went charging after the Portos, she said, "There could be a number of explanations for why Wyatt left his Jeep here."

"Name one."

"The woman he was going to see could have picked him up here. Maybe he took her to one of the clubs nearby or went with her in her car. You know Wyatt. He could be anywhere."

"I know Wyatt," John said, his voice grimly quiet as he reached into the Jeep and brought out a set of keys. "He wouldn't have left his keys in the Jeep."

Salem had been vainly hanging on to the hope that Wyatt had simply gone to one of the clubs. Yet she too knew Wyatt wouldn't have left his keys.

"Do you know the woman he's been seeing?" she asked.

Pocketing the keys, John locked the Jeep door and shut it firmly. "Cheryl something-or-other. If he ever said her last name, I can't remember what it is."

"Let's check the clubs first, just in case he went to one of them. He could have arranged to meet her somewhere close by. You take one side of the street and I'll take the other."

John took her arm, holding it firmly as he walked toward the street. "We stay together. I'm not letting you out of my sight. They might already have Wyatt. They aren't going to get their grimy hands on you too."

For two hours, they went from one nightclub to another, moving through the darkened interiors, scanning each table, each face. John's jaw was rigid with frustration and anger when they left the last club in the area. Salem knew he was going through hell wondering where Wyatt was, but there was nothing she could say to comfort him. She didn't suggest going to the police, as they had the same problem they'd had all along. There was no proof Wyatt had been forcibly taken from the parking lot, or that the Porto brothers were the ones responsible.

With purposeful strides, John drew her along with him to the parking lot where he had parked his own Jeep. First he drove to the address the phone book listed for the three Porto brothers. The lights of the Jeep illuminated a for-sale sign stuck in the middle of the lawn. It was one of the newer houses on the island, large and modern and in an expensive area. There were no cars in the drive, and not a single light shone through the windows.

John then drove to the marina where the Porto brothers kept their boat. There was no sign of activity on the boat or on the dock. A gate was stretched across the entrance to the dock, and a padlock and chain secured it to a sturdy post. The usual security lights were on at the end of the dock, but the boat was dark.

"Do they have more than one boat?" Salem asked.

"They did have three. Wyatt heard the other two were repossessed by the bank a couple of days ago."

Salem jumped when John struck the steering wheel with the palm of his hand. Since there was nothing she could say to ease his anger and frustration, she moved her hand to his thigh to let him know he wasn't alone.

He took a deep steadying breath and covered her hand with his. "I hate this, Salem. I hate feeling helpless. There has to be something I can do to find Wyatt before . . ."

He didn't finish what he was going to say, but she knew what he meant. Before Wyatt was injured or worse.

"Delta was right about one thing," she said. "We need to find out more about these men. There has to be something we've missed, some reason why they would take Wyatt away. If we knew more, maybe we could find out where they've taken Wyatt. Then we could figure out how to get him back."

"Do you remember the name of the realtor listed on the for-sale sign in front of their house?"

Nodding, Salem gave him the name, realizing why he wanted it. If the Portos were buying or renting, they would have filled out papers giving past addresses, perhaps next of kin, references. It was a start.

"It's after midnight," she said. "We'll have to wait until they open for business tomorrow."

As much as he hated to waste time doing nothing, he had to admit she was right. They could do nothing until morning. As soon as it was light, he would gather the crew together and have them thoroughly search the island while he went to the realty office, the licensing bureau, and the Coast Guard if necessary. He was going to find out everything possible about the three men who had been terrorizing his fleet. And who now had Wyatt. He didn't need proof. It was the only explanation. He was going to do what he should have done all along. Confront the bastards and have it out with them.

His fingers tightened on Salem's small hand. He'd been so wrapped up in finally claiming her, he hadn't followed through with an investigation of the Portos. He had treated their threat too lightly. It was his fault Wyatt might be in danger, and he would have to live with his guilt if anything happened to Wyatt.

He released her hand so he could start the engine and was irrationally pleased when she didn't move her hand off his thigh. Whatever happened, he was going to keep Salem with him. To hell with trying to do things right. Since when had he ever done anything according to the unwritten laws of society? All he'd accomplished by giving Salem the courtship he thought she deserved was to confuse her and drive himself crazy. Whether she, Delta, or the whole damn world liked it or not, she was going to be where he could see her. He couldn't take the chance of something happening to her too.

Instead of driving back to Delta's house, he drove to his cottage. He was past giving Salem a choice. Tonight he needed her with him.

He parked in front of the cottage, and they got out at the same time. He took her hand and led her to the front door. After unlocking the door and shoving it open, he made no move to enter. He reached inside and flicked on the hall light, then squinted at the crack in the door, trying to see if someone was hiding behind it.

Refusing to leave Salem on the doorstep even for the brief time it would take him to look around, he gently pushed her inside and shut the door behind them, locking it. Leaving Salem in the hall, he checked out the rest of the cottage until he was satisfied no one was there at the moment, nor had been there earlier.

Salem was closing the drapes in the front room

when he returned. Her movements were unusually lethargic as she walked over to one of the chairs where Wyatt's jacket lay crumpled on the cushion. She folded it and laid it over the back of the chair, her gaze remaining fixed on it.

"He'll be all right, Salem," he said quietly. "There's no reason for them to harm him."

She looked at him. "That's the problem, isn't it? There's no reason we can think of why these men have done any of the things they've done. None of it makes sense. But don't tell me they won't harm him, John. I'm not a child. They aren't playing games. They attacked you and two crewmen, and blew up the boat shed. Now they have Wyatt. They want something, and they aren't being too subtle about how they go about getting it."

He tore off his tie and shrugged out of his jacket. As much for himself as for her, he went to her and took her in his arms. "If we have to tear the entire island apart, we'll find him, honey. I promise you that. I've never broken a promise to you. I'm not going to start now."

She melted against him, sliding her hands around his firm waist. His scent was familiar, his body warm and hard against her softness. Desire coiled inside her, spiraling along her veins like red-hot lava.

Lifting her chin, he took her mouth with an avid kiss. Their need for each other was immediate and strong, so painfully intense it couldn't be denied. Fear for Wyatt's safety, the uncertainty of their new relationship, the passion throbbing between them—all combined to intensify their hunger to be together.

John's fingers were shaking as he undid the

buttons on the front of her dress. Parting the material, he slid his hands inside, needing to feel her bare skin. The dress slid down her arms, then tumbled to the floor. The lacy strip of cloth covering her breasts was discarded along with the rest of her clothing until she was naked in his arms.

When he felt her fingers at the buckle of his belt, he raised his head and looked down at her. Her lips were moist and parted as she met his hot gaze. She unfastened the front of his slacks and slid her hand inside.

He jerked when he felt her slim fingers stroke his sensitive hard flesh. Groaning hoarsely, he kissed her with a savage ferocity, his tongue surging into her as he began to tear off his shirt.

He couldn't wait to take her to his bedroom. Still kissing her, he lowered her to the carpet, covering her with his body. Lacing his fingers through hers, he held their hands above her head as he thrust into her.

She met him eagerly, enticing him, challenging him, joining him in the rush for the aching pleasure awaiting them. Soft sounds escaped her from deep in her throat, her gaze never leaving his face as she gave him the gift of herself.

They reached the pinnacle of satisfaction together, the world shattering around them.

Many minutes passed before John found the strength to raise his head from the scented hollow of her neck. Staring into her glowing eyes, he murmured, "I love you, Salem. I've loved the charming child from the orphanage, the beguiling adolescent, and the spirited teenager. But it's the woman you've become that I love now."

He saw her face pale as she gasped at him. Was it such a shock? he wondered with amazement.

He thought he'd been more than obvious about the way he felt about her.

A single tear escaped from the corner of her eye and rolled slowly down her cheek. "I love you too, John. I always have. Not as a big brother or a guardian. I'm in love with you." She arched her hips, her eyes changing when she felt him harden inside her. "Like this. You're a part of me."

Her softly spoken words shot through him like a thunderbolt, but her sensual movements blanked out everything but the need to make love to her. With a groan of wrenching pleasure, he bent his head and kissed her as she wrapped her arms around him.

Later, they fell asleep in his bed, exhausted and dazed. John's embrace was tender yet possessive through what was left of the night.

Dawn was just lightening the sky when Salem opened her eyes to find John awake beside her. His hand lay across her rib cage, and he was watching her intently.

"Hi," she said.

He smiled. "Good morning." His smile widened when she rubbed her eyes with her knuckles. "One advantage of knowing each other for a long time is that we don't have to worry about learning each other's habits." He drew her hand away from her eyes. "For instance, I know you need a shower before you're fully awake, so I'll make the coffee."

She would rather curl up in his arms and go back to sleep, she thought. "And you drink two cups, black, no sugar," she said. "What time is it? Never mind. I don't really want to know. We have to get up, don't we?"

His smile faded. "I'm afraid so. We have a lot of ground to cover." He kissed her. "When we get

Wyatt back safely, we'll take some time off. Just the two of us. How does that sound?"

Feeling as though she'd been granted a reprieve, she said solemnly, "It sounds wonderful."

With reluctance in every movement, he levered himself away from her and got out of bed. After finding clean underwear in the dresser, he turned to the closet. He tossed one of his shirts to her before taking one for himself and a pair of jeans.

As he zipped up his jeans, he glanced at the bed. She hadn't moved and was watching him. The thin sheet flowed over her body, barely concealing the tantalizing shape of her. Her hair was tousled on the pillow. His pillow. It was a sight he planned to see every morning for the rest of his life. His body instantly responded to the aching longing in her eyes.

"Salem," he said huskily, "go take a shower."

Blinking her eyes as though she were coming out of a trance, she threw back the covers and got up. She draped his shirt over her arm and walked toward the bathroom, unabashedly naked.

John closed his eyes against the shaft of sensual hunger jolting through him. Then he left his bedroom while he still could.

Later, when John was taking a shower, Salem found the pair of deck shoes she'd left behind several days before. Rummaging around in the closet, she also came up with a pair of gray track pants with a drawstring waist. After she slipped them on, she knotted the tail of his shirt at her waist. Her outfit wouldn't make a well-dressed list, but at least she was decently covered so she could get to Delta's.

Once Wyatt was safe, she mused, there were going to have to be a few changes in the way things were between her and John. She couldn't keep returning to Delta's in her previous day's clothes or whatever she could raid from John's closet. He said he loved her. And, she loved him desperately. The natural progression of events should be marriage. But he hadn't said anything about getting married, and she couldn't bring herself to mention it in case it wasn't what he wanted. Nor could she just move in with him. As badly as she wanted to be with him, she couldn't live with him without the benefit of marriage. She wanted a home, a husband, children, the whole traditional family life neither of them had ever had. She wouldn't settle for anything less and didn't want any less for John.

But first they had to find Wyatt.

Instead of having to drive around the island to find information about the Portos, they accomplished the same thing by sitting at the kitchen table at Delta's listening to Connie dial one number after another. When they arrived at Delta's so Salem could change clothes, John told Connie about the latest development. Her dark eyes glittered with black fire when she heard Wyatt had apparently been kidnapped. Without saying a word, she walked over to the wall phone and punched out a number, speaking to whoever answered in her own language.

She was still on the phone when Salem came down from her room. She looked at John with a question in her eyes, and he shrugged. After pouring herself a cup of coffee, she sat down at the table and waited with John. Since Connie was speaking in Haitian, Salem could only surmise she was talking to some of her relatives and friends. Off and on over the years, she had met a number of them and knew there was a large contingent of the Dubacca family living and working on the island.

Finally, Connie replaced the phone. "It is done. In perhaps an hour, we will know more."

John didn't doubt it for a moment. What did surprise him was he hadn't thought to use Connie's connections before. His gaze moved to the woman across the table. His only excuse was he'd had other things on his mind.

"While we're waiting," he said, "I want to talk to my crew. I'll send a couple of the men to watch the Portos' boat, another their house. The rest I want on standby in case we need them."

Connie nodded her agreement. "My brother and my cousins will also be ready to help if needed. Will you have breakfast before you leave? Battles are better fought on a full stomach."

John pushed his chair back. "We'll eat something later, Connie. When we have Wyatt back."

He looked down at Salem and held out his hand. "Come with me."

She placed her hand in his. She would gladly go with him, to the ends of the earth and beyond. All he had to do was ask.

An hour later they returned to Delta's to find Connie again on the phone. The crew was waiting by a ship's radio for word from John. All charters had been canceled. Every crew member was prepared to do whatever had to be done to get Wyatt back and to end the harassment.

Connie's relatives had come through. A piece of property on Stone Island was leased to Merlin Porto.

Unlike the main islands of the Florida Keys, Stone Island wasn't connected by the highway and bridges that extended 150 miles from the tip of mainland Florida. It was accessible only by the sea, which explained why the Portos' boat had been gone that morning.

John's first instinct was to charge immediately out to the island, but he knew Wyatt's safety depended on how he handled the rescue. Connie's younger brother had been part of the construction crew that had built the only house on the small island. Meeting John and his crew on the docks, he described the location in remarkable detail, then agreed to go with them to the island. They had no way of knowing for sure that Wyatt was being held there, but it was the only lead they had.

Along with the crew of the Gypsy Fleet, nine members of Connie's family were on hand to assist, which gave them a total of six men to each boat. They only man who was armed was a member of the local police force who happened to be Connie's brother-in-law.

Salem was beyond being surprised by the extent of Connie's help. She was just thankful the older woman had made it easier for them to find Wyatt. While John rolled up the chart they had all studied, she started to walk toward the *Gypsy I.* John called her back.

As she approached him, he said sternly, "You aren't going."

She lifted her chin. "Yes, I am." When he shook his head, she planted her hands on her hips. "I'm going, John."

"We don't know what's waiting for us out there, Salem. I want you to stay here where you'll be safe. If things get rough, I don't want to be worrying about you."

Salem was unaware of the attention they were receiving from the crew and raised her voice to match John's. "When the going's been rough in the past, I've never complained, have I? I've never asked for more than you and Wyatt had, and I've worked right along with both of you ever since we arrived here. I have a right to go with you. You don't need to worry about me. Wyatt is our first concern, our only concern. We're wasting time arguing."

Aside from physically restraining her, John knew he wouldn't be able to keep her from going to Stone Island. If he refused to take her with him, she would only find some other boat and go there herself.

He took her arm and started walking up the dock. "All right, but stay out of the way if things get out of hand," he growled.

Luckily, the sky was sunny and the water calm, without any sign of an impending storm. Staying together, the boats glided past some of the islands of the lower Keys. When they rounded the upper coast of Big Torch Key, the boats fanned out, two going south around the lower edge while the *Gypsy I* and another boat headed to the north. The plan was to come in from both sides of the island to reach the bay the house was located on.

Stone Island was small, covered with trees that edged up to the shoreline. They saw no sign of habitation until they reached the east side. In a small clearing a few hundred feet back from the shore sat a sprawling single-story house. A wooden dock extended out into the water. Tied up to the dock was the boat that belonged to the Porto brothers.

John shifted the throttle to neutral, and they drifted while they waited for the other two boats to come around from the other side of the island.

Standing beside John, Salem gazed at the house but was unable to see any sign of activity. Now that they were so close, she felt the unwelcome tingle of fear in her stomach.

"Do you think Wyatt is there?" she asked.

"I don't know," John said quietly. "We'll soon find out."

They saw the other two boats at the same time. John got on the radio and told them to remain off the coast. There wasn't enough room at the dock for all four boats to tie up. It was going to be tight as it was for the *Gypsy I* with the Portos' boat taking up nearly one side of the dock.

Instructing the skipper of the boat beside them to stay where he was, John pushed the throttle forward, a determined look in his eyes. With one hand on the wheel, he opened a small cabinet and removed a flare gun, tucking it into the waistband of his jeans at the back. If they ran into any trouble on shore, he would fire the flare gun.

As they tied up at the dock, Salem continued to watch the house, half expecting men to race out of it with weapons pointed at them. No one appeared.

Instructing one crew member to stay on board, John took Salem's hand. He'd rather she remained on board, too, but since she wouldn't, he was going to make sure she stayed with him. He could understand why she wanted to go along, but he also understood the necessity of keeping her safe. It was as vital to him as breathing.

With John leading and Salem beside him, the other three men fell in behind them as they walked off the dock and started up the wooden steps to the house. When they were closer, they could see the beginning of a tiled patio partially hidden by thick bushes. That side of the wood-frame house boasted a number of windows, but they still saw no one.

John's hand tightened around Salem's as he stepped onto the patio. When he saw the sight in front of him, he stopped and stared. Salem stared as well. Seated at a round wrought-iron table were three men she assumed were the Portos, Wyatt, and the red-haired woman from the gallery. Wyatt's hands were free. In one of them he was holding a glass of iced tea. There were no marks of violence on his face.

For a moment, no one moved or said anything. Clearly they were expected; there was no surprise on the Portos' faces. Or fear.

Slowly walking forward, John spoke to the man seated next to Wyatt. "What's going on, Frank? Why have you brought Wyatt here?"

Before the older man could answer, the red-headed woman glared at Salem and snapped, "What's she doing here? I want her away from here, Frank."

Frank ignored her outburst, answering John's questions instead. "Your partner is a very stubborn man. A great deal like you. Since you couldn't be persuaded to cooperate, we decided to try him. He wouldn't agree to sign over his half of the Gypsy Fleet or to marry my sister, so we brought him here until he does agree to both."

John wasn't surprised by Frank's saying he wanted Wyatt's share of the fleet, but the calm remark about Wyatt's marrying his sister floored him. He stared at Wyatt. "What's he talking about?"

"It seems their sister is pregnant. She's named me as the father."

"Are you?" John asked bluntly.

"No."

John shifted his gaze to Frank. "He's not going to sign over his share of the fleet, even if you kept him here for the rest of his life. Nor is he going to be forced into marrying a woman just because she says he's the father of her child. He's coming back with us."

The two other men rose from the table, their expressions angry. Frank held up his hand, which was enough to stop them from doing whatever they were going to do. "My sister would not lie about something this serious, Mr. Canada," he said calmly. "If she says your partner is responsible for her condition, then it is true."

The woman pointed at Salem. "It's all her fault. If she hadn't come to Key West, Wyatt would have come back to me. Get rid of her, Frank."

"Leave Salem out of this," Wyatt said. He shook his head wearily. "I've told you time and again, I've never even been out with your sister, Porto. I bought her a drink one night. That's all. If Maria's pregnant, it was some other man."

John took a step forward. "This is a pretty cheap way to blackmail Wyatt into signing over his half of the business, Porto. When the assaults on us and the boat shed didn't work, you used a fake pregnancy. It makes me wonder what you'll try next.

Frank's face flushed with anger. "My sister told me of her pregnancy two days ago. She named your partner. He will not disgrace her by leaving her to raise this child by herself." His angry gaze went to Salem. "You will have to give up your interest in Mr. Brodie, my dear. He will marry my sister if he values that pretty face of his."

Salem looked from Wyatt to the redheaded woman he had called Maria. Things were falling into place in her mind. Meeting the other woman's furious gaze, she asked, "Did you tell your brothers Wyatt was interested in me?"

Maria lifted her chin. "Of course I did. When you wouldn't take my warning, Merlin sent someone to your house to tell you to stay away from Wyatt. Now you're here to try to get him back, but he's mine!"

Salem heard the hysterical note in Maria's voice and was amazed her brothers didn't realize she had a tenuous grasp on reality. Since she couldn't hope to talk any sense into Maria, she turned to Frank. "I don't know where your sister got the idea I was romantically involved with Wyatt, but it's not true. I grew up with Wyatt. We're very close, but like a brother and sister. If she lied about my relationship with Wyatt, couldn't she be lying about her relationship with him?"

For the first time, Frank looked uncertain and hesitant. His gaze lowered to Salem's hand, held securely in John's. Raising his eyes to meet John's, he asked, "Is she your woman?"

"Yes."

Frank turned to his sister. "Maria, it seems you were wrong about there being another woman. I think—"

Maria must have believed she was losing her brother's support. She leapt to her feet so abruptly, her chair tipped over. "Are you going to believe them or your own sister?"

Her voice spiraled out of control. She raised her hand as though to strike Frank, but her other brothers rushed over to hold her. The moment she was restrained by their strong arms, she started ranting and raving like a small child having a tantrum. With a nod of Frank's head, his brothers took her into the house. Her screams could be heard even after the sliding glass door had been shut behind them.

Frank slowly pushed his chair back and stood up. "It seems I owe you an apology, Mr. Brodie. You are allowed to leave." He glanced at John. "I will not apologize for trying to ruin you. That's business."

John couldn't understand the other man's convoluted logic, but it didn't matter. Wyatt was standing on the other side of Salem. He'd gotten what he'd come for. "You're finished in Key West, Porto. You just haven't realized it yet. I could suggest you get some professional help for your sister, but I know it wouldn't do any good." His voice hardened. "If you ever attempt even to talk to either Wyatt or Salem in the future, I'll come after you. Alone. Just you and me. That's not a threat. That's a promise."

Still holding Salem's hand, John turned away and started back to the boat. When they stepped onto the dock, he felt Salem trying to move her fingers and realized he'd been holding her hand in a grip of steel. He loosened his hold on her but didn't let her go completely until she was safely aboard the boat.

He got on the radio as Wyatt started the engine and drew away from the dock. He told the other boats to return to the marina, that Wyatt was with them.

When he got off the radio, he looked around for Salem but didn't see her. The only place she could be was down in the cabin. Leaving Wyatt at the helm, he went down there. She was at the sink getting a glass of water.

He waited until she'd finished before speaking. "I feel like a general who made elaborate battle plans, then had the war called off. All my precautions seem a little silly now."

"You had no way of knowing how they were going to react when we arrived or what they would do to Wyatt. I hope they realize their sister needs professional help. She's caused a lot of problems with her accusations."

"Why didn't you tell me that crazy woman warned you off Wyatt?"

Salem set the glass down and turned to face him. "Because I thought she was referring to you."

Ten

John stared at her. "Why would you think that?"

"She didn't mention Wyatt by name. Just that she had been shoved aside when I returned to Key West. Since I was involved with you and not Wyatt, it was logical to think she meant you. She was also wearing a gold medalion similar to mine."

John smiled faintly. "I don't go around handing out gold coins to every woman on the island, Salem." He took the one step that brought him next to her. Raising his hand, he stroked the back of his fingers over her jaw line. "I'm not going to lie to you and say there haven't been other women in the past, but none of them meant anything other than a brief sexual encounter. I've never slept an entire night with any woman but you. I've never made love with any woman but you. Sex, but not love."

His touch was having its usual effect on her. "I wasn't asking if there were other women, John."

"I would feel more secure if you did." He saw

her eyes widen in surprise. "I was jealous as hell when you told me in Seattle that you had dated other men and had become more experienced. The thought of another man making love to you nearly drove me over the edge. I would like to think you don't like the idea of me being with another woman any more than I like the thought of you being with another man."

"We were estranged for four years, John. You said I was too young for you, that I didn't know who I was. You were determined not to become physically involved with me. I knew there was a possibility you would be with other women."

He frowned. There was a strange note of bitterness in her voice when she said that about not knowing who she was. Before he could question her about what she meant, he felt the revolutions of the engine slowing down. They were approaching the dock.

"We're coming in. I have to talk to the crew and Connie's relatives before I can leave. They'll want to know what happened. Why don't you go back to Delta's." He took his keys out of his pocket and handed them to her. "Take my Jeep. I'll meet you there later." He brought this hand up to cup her neck. "Maybe now things can get back to the way they were."

Salem nodded and remained where she was while John went up on deck, his words ringing in her ears. He was hoping they could continue as they had before.

She was relieved he hadn't been involved with that woman, but there were still other factors between her and John that weren't resolved. And might never be. She was running out of time before she had to give the company in Monterey her answer. If John didn't want to make their relationship permanent, she would have to leave Key West. If she stayed, she knew they would continue to be lovers. The chemistry between them was too strong to be denied or ignored. Nor could she stay at Delta's indefinitely, living off the other woman's kindness.

She kept telling John she was no longer a child but an independent woman. It was about time she acted like one. If there was to be no future with John, the future she wanted with him, then it was time to make the break. The longer she stayed, the harder it would be to leave.

Once the boat was tied up, she left the cabin. John and Wyatt were walking up the dock toward shore where some of the other crew members waited for them. She saw the circle of men open to swallow the two of them, and Wyatt's back was slapped several times. She walked on past them.

When she arrived at Delta's, she found Connie in the garden behind the house and told her what had happened. The cook handed her the wooden basket with vegetables for the evening meal and continued to move down the rows of plants, occasionally nodding her head as she listened.

As she carried the vegetables into the house, Salem envied the older woman's serenity. Very little seemed to bother Connie, no matter what the circumstances. The woman was content with her life, secure in her position in Delta's home, comfortable with herself and those around her.

While Salem was washing the vegetables at the kitchen sink, Connie said, "There was a phone call for you today from California. I wrote down the number on the pad next to the phone. They would like you to call them back as soon as possible."

Drying her hands, Salem picked up the pad and recognized the name Connie had jotted down, that of the director of personnel at the marine museum in Monterey. She glanced at the clock above the phone. Because of the time difference, the museum should still be open.

Still she hesitated to call. The director was waiting for a decision, and she didn't have one to give him. The job was the best offer she'd had. The pay would be more than adequate to support herself, and there was a chance for advancement. She would be a fool to turn it down. As she began to punch out the numbers, she knew that was exactly what she was going to do. She didn't want to go to California. She wanted to stay in Key West with John.

There was a short delay before the director came on the line. She was about to tell him she was turning down the job when he said, "We received a letter of reference from Mr. Canada. He spoke very highly of your diving training and experience. Along with your other qualifications, we feel you will be a—"

"When did Mr. Canada write the letter?" Salem interrupted.

There was a brief rustling of papers in the background, then the director read off the date. The letter had been written two days after she and John had become lovers. Why was she surprised that he still thought she would take the job? she wondered sadly. All along he had told various people she was going to Monterey.

"In our original offer," the director went on, "we specified we would like you to start work in September, but we have a new project we're working on that could use your experience as a diver. We want to try some experiments on the kelp beds, and they will need to be checked daily. That's why we need qualified divers. We were hoping you could start the beginning of July."

That was only two weeks away, she realized. "How soon do you have to have my decision?"

"I would like it as soon as possible. We want to get the schedule approved and everything in place so we can get started this summer while the weather is suitable for diving."

Her hand tightened around the receiver. "I'll give you my answer tomorrow."

The director agreed, and Salem replaced the phone and slowly turned around. Connie was making no pretense of working. She was watching Salem, her hands on her hips, a frown on her face.

"Why didn't you give him an answer now?"

"I don't know what it will be."

"You belong here, child. We all want you to stay."

Salem smiled wanly. "I'll find out tonight whether or not that's true."

John and Wyatt arrived in time for dinner, which included Delta, Connie, and Salem.

Delta was pleased to have her little family to herself and said as much. "I have decided not to accept any more guests. It's too much work for Connie, and I've discovered I like having the house to ourselves."

Everyone, including Connie, stared at her. For as long as Salem had known Delta, she had always had houseguests. Delta smiled at their concerned faces and waved her hand in a dismissive gesture. "It's not that unusual for a woman of my advanced age to want to take life a little easier. In fact, I've been considering selling the house and studio if I can find a smaller place. Maybe an apartment. Once Salem leaves, there will just be Connie and I rattling around in this big old house."

In unison, John, Wyatt, and Connie turned their heads to look at Salem, their expressions registering their shock at Delta's announcements. Salem continued to stare at Delta.

John's eyes narrowed as he stared at Salem. Even though they hadn't discussed it, he really hadn't expected her to leave. "What does she mean, 'once you leave'?"

Salem slowly turned her head and met his angry gaze. He was sitting back in his chair, appearing calm and relaxed, but she could see the pulse throbbing in his neck. "The director of the museum in Monterey phoned. They want me to start earlier than September. He also said he'd received a letter of recommendation from you. I suppose I should thank you. It was your letter that made him want me to start earlier."

"I didn't realize you'd decided to take the job," he said quietly.

She lowered her gaze to the table, her fingers fiddling with her knife and spoon. "Well, actually I haven't. I told the director I would give him an answer tomorrow." She looked up at him again. "You've been telling everyone all along that I'm going to take the job, as though it were an accomplished fact. I wouldn't want to make you out to be a liar."

She was waiting for him to tell her he wanted her to stay. All he had to do was say he didn't want her to go.

A muscle clenched in his jaw. Without saying another word, he pushed back his chair and left the table. When Salem heard the front door slam, she shoved her own chair back.

"Excuse me," she murmured, and escaped the room.

Wyatt sighed heavily. "This love stuff is a pain in the butt."

Delta laughed. "But it's the best game in town." She reached over and patted his hand. "Don't worry. John won't let her leave. All he needed was a little push. Left to his own devices, he would have continued to drift along in his relationship with Salem."

Wyatt's eyes narrowed as he met Delta's amused gaze. Comprehension gradually dawned. "You made that up about selling the house, didn't you."

"Well, of course, dear boy. What would I do in a dinky apartment? I wanted Salem to believe she wouldn't have anyplace to return to if she did decide to take the job so far away. John can't waffle around without making a commitment now, because Salem has to give her answer to the marine place by tomorrow. Sometimes people need a push in the direction they wanted to go in the first place."

Whistling under his breath, Wyatt shook his head in bemusement. "Being a mere man, I can't fathom the thinking behind your plot. I just hope it works."

Delta smiled complacently. "If nothing else, it's certainly been interesting since Salem came back."

*　　*　　*

A little before dawn, Salem finally managed to close her eyes, her body forcing her mind to shut down so she could get some sleep. Hours of pacing her bedroom, then staring at the ceiling, hadn't accomplished a thing except to wear her out.

Little breezes wafted in through the open window. She'd thrown the sheet and light blanket off her, her oversized T-shirt the only covering she needed.

She didn't hear the door open or wake when light from the hall illuminated the room. John stepped inside, closing the door partway so there was just enough light for him to see the furniture. His gaze automatically went to the occupant of the bed. She was lying on her side, her face turned away from him. Her T-shirt barely covered her tantalizing feminine bottom, giving him a clear view of the soft flesh he loved.

He sucked in his breath as heat seared across his loins. With rigid control, he pulled his thoughts away from the tempting woman on the bed and stepped over to the chest of drawers. Carefully sliding the top drawer open, he took out a couple of silky pieces of undergarments and slipped them into the canvas satchel he'd brought with him. Then he went to the closet and rummaged around inside before sliding a few items of clothing off their hangers. Folding them neatly, he stuffed them in the satchel, along with a pair of sandals he spotted on the floor of the closet. He'd already taken some of her toiletries out of the bathroom, just the basic necessities—toothbrush, hairbrush, and her robe hanging on the back of the door.

Sliding the canvas strap over his shoulder, he crossed the room to the other side of the bed. Her small slender hand was spread out on the pillow, her cheek resting against it. Fourteen years ago, he'd stood by her bed looking down at her as she slept. She'd come willingly with him then. He wasn't so sure she would now.

Sliding one arm under her neck, the other under her thighs, he lifted her. She made a soft sound of protest, but she didn't awaken. Holding her tightly, he carried her across the room, using his foot to open the door wider. The canvas satchel thumped dully against the frame of the door as he turned sideways to maneuver her through the doorway. Unlike the other time, he didn't have to worry about creaking stairs giving him away. His deck shoes made no sound at all on the carpeted steps as he carried her down.

He'd left the front door ajar, so it required only a nudge of his foot to open it further. Salem shivered in his arms as the cooler predawn air flowed over her warm skin. He quickened his pace to the Jeep. He wanted her out of the house before she awoke, although it wouldn't have made any difference if she'd been awake when he'd entered her room. She was coming with him if he had to carry her out kicking and screaming.

Their courtship was over.

Her heavy eyelids fluttered open when he set her in the front seat of the Jeep. Her voice was low and drowsy as she murmured his name, sending a frisson of reaction along his veins.

He leaned down and touched her mouth with his, all too briefly. She responded instantly, and he had to check himself from giving in to the need to kiss her again.

He started to move away from her, but her arms encircled his neck as she parted her lips to deepen the kiss. He groaned as her tongue brushed against his, igniting the barely banked fires within him.

"Salem," he whispered. "As much as I would like to continue this, we have things to do first."

"Like what?"

He looked down at her. "Fourteen years ago, you trusted me enough to come away with me from the orphanage. I want you to come with me now."

Her eyes searched his for a long moment. Then she lowered her hands from his neck and reached for the seat belt. When it clicked into place, she clasped her hands lightly in her lap and smiled at him.

Feeling disoriented from the love and trust in her eyes and her smile, he gently shut the door and walked in a daze around the Jeep. As it had so long ago, her trust touched him deeply.

Salem didn't ask a single question as he drove. When he parked at the dock, she got down from the Jeep and waited while he took a canvas satchel out of the back. Walking beside him toward the dock, she was relieved—considering how she was dressed—to see there wasn't a crewman guarding the boats.

John boarded the *Gypsy I* first, then turned to give her his hand to help her aboard. The breeze off the Gulf tore at the thin material of her T-shirt, plastering it to the front of her body.

He handed her the satchel. "Go below," he said, his voice oddly hoarse, "and put on some warmer clothes. I'll be up on the fly bridge after I untie the lines."

Vibrant colors across the sky were announcing the arrival of another sunrise when Salem climbed the ladder to the fly bridge. She'd found a pair of jeans, a shirt, and a sweater in the satchel and had put them on. The wind tousled John's dark hair as he looked down to take a compass reading, one hand holding the wheel easily. She knew this was his favorite time, early morning before the sun appeared in full force. Each dawn was the beginning of a new day, and she was happy just to be with him, even though she had no idea what the day would bring.

He turned his head and met her gaze. As she walked toward him, he lifted his hand to her. His hard fingers curled around her hand, drawing her closer. He positioned her in front of him, her back pressed against him, and they stood watching the sun rise as the boat cleaved the sea.

She had no idea where they were going and didn't particularly care. If this was his way of saying good-bye, she vowed she would enjoy whatever time was left to her and wouldn't beg for more.

As they neared one of the small uninhabited islands that made up the chain of the Keys, John slowed the engine. A few minutes later they entered a sheltered cove. He cut the engine and pressed a button to lower the anchor.

With his hands on her shoulders, he turned her. "How do you feel about an early morning swim?"

She flicked a glance at the section of beach about fifty yards from the boat. "To the island?"

He nodded. "To the island."

Without waiting for her to answer, he started down the ladder. When he reached the deck, he kicked off his shoes and looked up at her. "Are you coming?"

John didn't dive into the water until she reached the deck. Salem removed her deck shoes and pulled the thick sweater over her head, letting it fall to the deck. As he had, she left her jeans and shirt on, then dove into the water and began to swim toward shore.

John was waiting for her in the shallow water lapping the shoreline. He took her hand and brought her against him, kissing her hungrily, his hands flowing over her. He licked the salt off her lips, then kissed her once more. When he finally raised his head, his eyes were blazing with desire, but he didn't kiss her again. Taking her hand, he led her into the trees lining the shore. Completely baffled, Salem kept her gaze on the ground, stepping over fallen branches and plants in their path. When he stopped walking, she looked up and saw a clearing where there was a tent and a lighted lantern hanging from the branch of one of the trees.

"When did you do all this?"

"During the night." He stepped over to the lantern and extinguished the flame. Now that the sun was coming up, they no longer needed the artificial light. "It was the only place I could think of where we wouldn't be interrupted."

He ducked into the tent, coming out a few seconds later with a large thick towel. His mouth curved in a sensual smile as he slowly walked toward her.

"You're all wet."

"So are you."

He began to dry her face with the towel, then her throat, his touch sparking a warm glow inside her. His gaze remained on her face as he said quietly, "I don't want you to go to Monterey."

She gazed at him in confusion. "Then why did you keep telling everyone I was going to take the job?"

"I told myself it had to be your decision. You were always telling me you were an adult and could make up your mind. I was hoping you would decide your place is here in the Keys with me."

She couldn't think straight when he was so near and took several steps away. "You've taught me many things over the years. How to swim, how to pilot a boat, how to drive a car, how to survive. But you've never taught me how to be a mistress. I don't think I'd be very good at it."

His hot gaze drilled into her. He could feel his heart pounding in his chest, the dry acrid taste of fear in his mouth. "How about a wife?"

He had only a few seconds to prepare himself before she launched herself into his arms. The towel fell unheeded to the ground. The pain in his wrist was nothing compared to the rush of pure joy as he held her locked against him. He turned around and around with her in his arms, feeling as though he'd been given his life back after wavering on the brink of eternal emptiness.

He rained kisses over her face, his mouth finally settling on hers. They were both breathing heavily when he lifted his head.

"I want you to be happy, Salem. If you want to go to work for the Miami group, I won't mind as long as you do it here in the Keys. When the children come, we might have to make a few adjustments, but we can work it out. Being a marine biologist is part of who you are. I don't think you should give it up."

Suddenly she stiffened in his arms. When she felt his hold slacken, she moved back enough to see his face clearly. "I know you don't like it that I don't have any background, John, but I will be a good mother and wife. I swear I will."

He blinked. "What in hell are you talking about?"

"You said in Seattle that I didn't know who I was. It's true, neither one of us knows who our parents are, but that isn't something either of us can change. Our children will have honorary aunts in Delta and Connie, and an uncle in Wyatt. That's more than we had."

He closed the distance between them and gripped her arms almost painfully, holding her in front of him. "Dammit, Salem, I wasn't talking about your background. I meant you were so young, you hadn't had a chance to know yourself yet. I don't give a damn if your father was Jack the Ripper and your mother was Lizzie Borden. I love you. You. The bewitching gypsy child, the dazzling woman. You'll drive me crazy at least twice a day, but I don't want to go on without you."

Her throat was choked with emotion, making it impossible for her to speak. She lifted her hands to his chest, then slid them over his shoulders to circle his neck. Rising up on her toes, she kissed him, loving his immediate response.

For a long moment John reveled in the feel of her, the taste of her, until he needed more. She was his, and he wanted to show her how much he loved her.

His lips still against hers, he repeated what he'd said earlier. "You're all wet."

Her eyes twinkled with a sensual glow. "My clothes are on the boat. Do you think I should go back for them?"

His fingers went to the buttons of her shirt. "You won't need them for a while."

Her hands went to the snap of his jeans. "How long is 'a while'?"

He lowered his head. "How about forever?"

She sighed as she gave herself to the current heating her blood. "That just might be long enough."

THE EDITOR'S CORNER

As you look forward to the holiday season—the most romantic season of all—you can plan on enjoying some of the very best love stories of the year from LOVESWEPT. Our authors know that not all gifts come in boxes wrapped in pretty paper and tied with bows. In fact, the most special gifts are the gifts that come from the heart, and in each of the six LOVESWEPTs next month, characters are presented with unique gifts that transform their lives through love.

Whenever we publish an Iris Johansen love story, it's an event! In **AN UNEXPECTED SONG,** LOVE-SWEPT #438, Iris's hero, Jason Hayes, is mesmerized by the lovely voice of singer Daisy Justine and realizes instantly that she was born to sing his music. But Daisy has obligations that mean more to her than fame and fortune. She desperately wants the role he offers, but even more she wants to be touched, devoured by the tormented man who tangled his fingers in her hair. Jason bestows upon Daisy the gift of music from his soul, and in turn she vows to capture his heart and free him from the darkness where he's lived for so long. This hauntingly beautiful story is a true treat for all lovers of romance from one of the genre's premier authors.

In **SATURDAY MORNINGS,** LOVESWEPT #439, Peggy Webb deals with a different kind of gift, the gift of belonging. To all observers, heroine Margaret Leigh Jones is a proper, straitlaced librarian who seems content with her life—until she meets outrageous rogue Andrew McGill when she brings him her poodle to train. Then she wishes she knew how to flirt instead of how to blush! And Andrew's

(continued)

peaceful Saturday mornings are never the same after Margaret Leigh learns a shocking family secret that sends her out looking for trouble and for ways to hone her womanly wiles. All of Andrew's possessive, protective instincts rush to the fore as he falls head over heels for this crazy, vulnerable woman who tries just a bit too hard to be brazen. Through Andrew's love Margaret Leigh finally sees the error of her ways and finds the answer to the questions of who she really is and where she belongs—as Andrew's soul mate, sharing his Saturday mornings forever.

Wonderful storyteller Lori Copeland returns next month with another lighthearted romp, 'TIZ THE SEASON, LOVESWEPT #440. Hero Cody Benderman has a tough job ahead of him in convincing Darby Piper that it's time for her to fall in love. The serious spitfire of an attorney won't budge an inch at first, when the undeniably tall, dark, and handsome construction foreman attempts to turn her orderly life into chaos by wrestling with her in the snow, tickling her breathless beside a crackling fire—and erecting a giant holiday display that has Darby's clients up in arms. But Darby gradually succumbs to Cody's charm, and she realizes he's given her a true gift of love—the gift of discovering the simple joys in life and taking the time to appreciate them. She knows she'll never stop loving or appreciating Cody!

LOVESWEPT #441 by Terry Lawrence is a sensuously charged story of UNFINISHED PASSION. Marcie Courville and Ray Crane meet again as jurors on the same case, but much has changed in the ten years since the ruggedly sexy construction worker had awakened the desire of the pretty, privi-

(continued)

leged young woman. In the intimate quarters of the jury room, each feels the sparks that still crackle between them, and each reacts differently. Ray knows he can still make Marcie burn with desire—and now he has so much more to offer her. Marcie knows she made the biggest mistake of her life when she broke Ray's heart all those years ago. But how can she erase the past? Through his love for her, Ray is able to give Marcie a precious gift—the gift of rectifying the past—and Marcie is able to restore the pride of the first man she ever loved, the only man she ever loved. Rest assured there's no unfinished passion between these two when the happy ending comes!

Gail Douglas makes a universal dream come true in **IT HAD TO BE YOU,** LOVESWEPT #442. Haven't you ever dreamed of falling in love aboard a luxury cruise ship? I can't think of a more romantic setting than the *QE2*. For Mike Harris it's love at first sight when he spots beautiful nymph Caitlin Grant on the dock. With her endless legs and sea-green eyes, Caitlin is his male fantasy come true—and he intends to make the most of their week together at sea. For Caitlin the gorgeous stranger in the Armani suit seems to be a perfect candidate for a shipboard romance. But how can she ever hope for more with a successful doctor who will never be able to understand her wanderer's spirit and the joy she derives from taking life as it comes? Caitlin believes she is following her heart's desire by traveling and experiencing life to the fullest—until her love for Mike makes her realize her true desire. He gives her restless heart the gift of a permanent home in his arms—and she promises to stay forever.

(continued)

Come along for the ride as psychologist Maya Stephens draws Wick McCall under her spell in **DEEPER AND DEEPER**, LOVESWEPT #443, by Jan Hudson. The sultry-eyed enchantress who conducts the no-smoking seminar has a voice that pours over Wick like warm honey, but the daredevil adventurer can't convince the teacher to date a younger man. Maya spends her days helping others overcome their problems, but she harbors secret terrors of her own. When Wick challenges her to surrender to the wildness beneath the cool facade she presents to the world, she does, reveling in his sizzling caresses and drowning in the depths of his tawny-gold eyes. For the first time in her life Maya is able to truly give of herself to another—not as a teacher to a student, but as a woman to a man, a lover to her partner—and she has Wick to thank for that. He's shown her it's possible to love and not lose, and to give everything she has and not feel empty inside, only fulfilled.

Enjoy next month's selection of LOVESWEPTs, while you contemplate what special gifts from the heart you'll present to those you love this season!

Sincerely,

Susann Brailey

Susann Brailey
Editor
LOVESWEPT
Bantam Books
666 Fifth Avenue
New York, NY 10103

FOREVER LOVESWEPT
SPECIAL KEEPSAKE EDITION OFFER
SELECTION FORM

Choose from these special Loveswepts by your favorite authors. Please write a 1 next to your first choice, a 2 next to your second choice. Loveswept will honor your preference as inventory allows.

♡ ♡ ♡ *Loveswept* ®

_____	BAD FOR EACH OTHER	Billie Green
_____	NOTORIOUS	Iris Johansen
_____	WILD CHILD	Suzanne Forster
_____	A WHOLE NEW LIGHT	Sandra Brown
_____	HOT TOUCH	Deborah Smith
_____	ONCE UPON A TIME...GOLDEN	
	THREADS	Kay Hooper

Attached are 15 hearts and the selection form which indicates my choices for my special hardcover Loveswept "Keepsake Edition." Please mail my book to:

NAME:_____

ADDRESS:_____

CITY/STATE:_____ZIP:_____